Nick Trenton grew up as a farm boy in rural Illinois in USA. He obtained a BS in Economics, followed by an MA in Behavioral Psychology.

Nick likes to say that he has become a professional expert at one of his favorite hobbies: people-watching. He is an accomplished skier and dreams of travelling the world and hosting a food show like Anthony Bourdain. He currently lives in Chicago, Illinois.

Other titles by Nick Trenton,
published by Manjul/Amaryllis

the over-thinking cure

How to Stay in the Present, Shake Negativity, and Stop Your Stress and Anxiety

Nick Trenton

AMARYLLIS
An imprint of Manjul Publishing House

AMARYLLIS
An imprint of Manjul Publishing House Pvt. Ltd.
• C-16, Sector 3, Noida, Uttar Pradesh 201 301, India
Website: www.manjulindia.com
Registered Office:
• 2nd Floor, Usha Preet Complex, 42 Malviya Nagar,
Bhopal 462 003 – India
Distribution Centres
Ahmedabad, Bengaluru, Chennai, Hyderabad,
Kochi, Kolkata, Mumbai, Noida, Pune

English translation rights arranged with PKCS Mind, Inc.
through TLL Literary Agency

This paperback edition first published in 2023
Tenth impression 2026

ISBN 978-93-5543-318-3

Printed and bound in India by Repro India Limited

Contents

CHAPTER 1

It's All in the Perspective

Being Proactive Versus Reactive

Life is 10% what happens to you and
90% how you deal with it.
– John Maxwell

People who are cool, calm, and collected just have something about them: What is the X factor that lets them remain so composed and in control of themselves? While overly anxious people flap around and freak out, calm people seem to be inhabiting an entirely different mindset. Let's begin this book by looking more closely at exactly what this mindset is, and how you can go about cultivating it in yourself.

Here's an interesting question: Who is in control of your life?

There are two main answers: Either you see something or someone else as responsible for what happens to you, or you see yourself as the primary agent, mainly responsible for how your life plays out. Proactive people are those who, in essence, do not depend on the environment to guide and shape their life, but rather take active responsibility and do things on their own. They focus on their scope of action, on what they want, and on how they can bring those things about. Naturally, their attitude puts them in a frame of mind that focuses on solving problems and seeking opportunities. Broadly, when it comes to their life path, they are the ones calling the shots.

Compare this to the opposite: someone who is reactive. As the name suggests, this is a person who acts only as a response to other people's actions, or according to the environment, and less from their own innate agency and desire. This is a more passive, more conditional, and more dependent position. It's more about what you "should" do or are being made to do, than what you genuinely want to do. Blame, indecisiveness, victimhood, people-pleasing powerlessness, and lack of responsibility all belong to this mindset, as well as the belief that other people can make you feel certain emotions or force you to do something.

Now, I know what you're thinking—surely it's impossible to be truly proactive? After all, none of us is one hundred percent in control of our lives. This is true. Being proactive, however, doesn't necessarily mean you always get your way; rather, it's an orientation of mind and an attitude that says, "*I can learn from mistakes. I can use my potential. I can try something new.*" In fact, a proactive person is also able to recognize when they don't actually have an influence over outcomes, and they can comfortably relinquish control.

So, it's not that being proactive means you are entitled and enabled to make the world exactly as you like it; rather, it means that you have conscious awareness of your own scope of action, you have an "internal locus of control," and you are willing to actively engage with obstacles and mistakes rather than passively assuming you have no control or responsibility. It's not really the outcome or result that matters, but the attitude.

Because a proactive person knows that they are in charge of their actions, their feelings, and their inner interpretations, they make efforts to create situations that actually align with their values. A reactive person quietly hopes that things will align for them, or that others will help them, or else they quietly resent when this doesn't happen or resort to blame.

Proactive people consciously *create* the conditions they desire, and they know that they are the only ones who are empowered to do so. This takes a degree of mindful awareness, honesty, and courage. It also means they have to be mature enough to shoulder some risk—if they fail, they know that only they are responsible and they can blame nobody.

Let's return to the question: Who is in control of your life? Well, it depends on you! You can *choose* to be in control of your own life, or you can forfeit that choice to others. The thing is, nobody can force you to take charge of your own life—you either embrace that agency or you fail to embrace it.

Now, what does all this have to do with cultivating an attitude of inner calm? As you can probably guess, those who are calm and composed tend to act from a proactive mindset. They feel calm because they are self-assured and confident in their own agency. They're not anxious in situations because they know that someone is in control—them! Because they have fully claimed their agency, they know that they always have options, they can always become aware of them and make conscious choices, and they can always make the best of even the worst possible outcomes.

When you are reactive, you have no such inner security. You are waiting for others to determine your fate, or sitting ineptly and complaining about what they choose for you. This is an innately anxious position. You are at the mercy of other people's actions—what could be more stressful than that? Because you doubt or ignore your own ability to take responsibility or find solutions, you may feel that there really aren't any solutions until someone or something else comes and provides them. Instead of feeling competent and filled with optimism or hope, you are naturally pessimistic and always on guard for the next bit of trouble.

So, if we want to be genuinely calmer and more relaxed people, how can we start moving toward a proactive rather than reactive mindset?

Drop Blaming and Complaining

> **Reactive**: Look at all these things and people and situations that aren't the way I want them to be . . .
>
> **Proactive**: What is the way that I want things to be, and how am ***I*** going to do make that happen?

When you complain, you are putting yourself in reactive mode. You are communicating to yourself and others that you are not responsible, and you relinquish your agency in favor of someone else's. One way to be more proactive is to get positively ruthless with the bad habit of complaining. Nothing good ever comes of complaining! You may think you feel a bit better after whining about something you're unhappy with, but all you do is disempower yourself further (and probably bore others).

This takes a bit of awareness. Be honest if you notice yourself ranting and moaning about things, and just stop dead in your tracks. Then ask yourself one important question:

What action can I take here?

This puts you in active, problem-solving mode. Stop waiting for someone to come and save you; think of ways to help yourself. If you can act, then act. If you don't like something, have the courage to change it or remove yourself from the situation. Think of it this way: *Not* acting is also a choice, and if you remain in a situation you don't like, what does that say?

If you can't act, well, you can still proactively choose your attitude. You can choose not to respond at all. Just because you find a situation uncomfortable doesn't mean you have to complain—or worse, look for someone to blame. How you react to circumstances is far, far more important than the circumstances themselves. You might not be able to take conscious action or do much about a situation, but you still have plenty of power over what you focus on, how you interpret the situation, the attitude you commit to having, the words you say, and the way you respond. You always have options. When you complain, however, you shut your eyes to those options and get stuck on the fact of your discomfort or annoyance.

Blame is harmful for the same reason—why hand your power over to someone else? Being in the victim role may feel good in the short term, but when we complain about how others act, we are forgetting one crucial piece of information: We, too, have the option to act. Blame can sometimes come from unconscious expectations or a feeling of entitlement. If you catch yourself blaming someone, it's time to get honest—are you expecting them to take charge of a problem that's not really theirs to fix? If they are genuinely in the wrong (it happens!), then ask yourself this: Does your being angry and indignant get you any closer to what you really want? It can be very freeing to realize that we don't have to control others to get them to behave in the ways we want—we can act directly ourselves, for ourselves. This instantly releases anxiety and self-doubt and helps us feel calm.

The Key to Calm, Focused Flexibility—Be Responsive, Not Reactive

> **Reactive**: Change is scary and threatening, so I'd better hunker down and ward it off.
>
> **Proactive**: I trust myself to engage with change productively, and welcome the ways it can help me evolve.

As we said, you always have options. True, sometimes you don't have very many, or you might not like the ones you have, but you are never a victim to circumstance and can always step up and take responsibility for your experience. Whether proactive or reactive, change will come. Life is filled with change, but we can adopt different postures in response. When we respond (not react), we engage dynamically and consciously with people and things around us. We answer life according to our own values and principles, and have a conversation with elements in our environment rather than taking orders from it like a slave or shutting it out completely!

As the old saying goes: Brittle things break before they bend. Just because you know who you are and take sure, conscious steps to making your own life doesn't mean you're rigid or uncompromising. In fact, you are a pro at adjusting and adapting. You evolve, you try things, you fail, you change your strategy, you try again.

You are curious about the new, not fearful of it. This is what allows you to grow and improve. It's not that you are a control freak; rather, you are always aware of the fact that you have a choice. Instead of fearfully clinging to what you know, you embrace novelty, explore, create, and take risks. The irony is that it's this way of living that is actually easier and less anxiety-provoking.

Nip "If Only" in the Bud

> **Reactive**: One day, I'm going to XYZ, if such-and-such happens, and then maybe . . . and then I hope . . .
>
> **Proactive**: I am taking steps toward the things I want to create for myself—*right now.*

Anxiety is often characterized by overthinking, rumination, and endless, pointless "what if" thoughts. In the reactive mindset, we dwell in this same space. We say things like:

> "If I had a little more cash right now, then . . ."
>
> "If I had a better family upbringing . . ."
>
> "One day I'll finally start my big dream . . ."
>
> "Just as soon as the winter is over, I think I'm going to . . ."

Really, these are nothing more than flimsy excuses and daydreams that go precisely nowhere. It's mental activity that never materializes into anything valuable in the real world—and that's a few short steps away from anxiety and worry. Commit to not using "if" or "one day" in this way. If you're honest, you'll see that behind this language is often procrastination, fear, avoidance, or the quiet hope that someone else is going to rush in one day and rescue your life for you.

Obviously, nobody is suggesting that you abandon making big dreams for yourself. However, if you are engaging in daydreaming *instead of* taking active steps in life to create what you want, you're doing yourself a disservice. Dreams and blue-sky thinking are there to inspire and fuel purposeful action—without action, they are just pleasant stories you tell yourself that leave you in exactly the same position as you started.

In that spirit, let's condense some of this down into practical steps we can take right now.

No More Blaming or Complaining

Whining about the weather. Gossiping about that person at work who annoys you. Listing a family member's faults to another family member. Going on a ten-minute rant to a friend about how mad you are to get that speeding fine you didn't deserve. And on and on. We all do it.

The first step is to become aware. Whenever you notice yourself complaining or blaming someone, literally imagine a giant red stop sign in your mind's eye and tell yourself to stop. Create a moment of space. In that space, become aware of the fact that you have a choice. Then, choose to answer this question: What action can I take? Breathe deeply and carry on, noticing how much calmer and in control you feel.

You could keep a complaints journal where you record all your misgivings, but under the condition that everything that you write down in there must be addressed at the end of the day. You need to take one concrete action toward resolving the issue. You'll soon train yourself to see how pointless complaining is and empower yourself in the process.

No More Reacting, Only Responding

Actively notice what causes you to feel anxious or out of control. Pause and write these down somewhere. For example, "I might lose my job at the end of the year." Once you've put your fears down on paper, look at them and acknowledge them.

Acknowledge how you feel about them. Then, take action. Underneath, write down as many options and opportunities you can identify. If you find yourself focusing on something else that worries or frightens you, write it on a separate page and repeat the process, finding potential options for *that* worry, too.

You'll find that deliberately training your mind toward choices and potential solutions actually calms you down, empowers you, and maybe even gets you excited for new ventures.

No More Daydreaming, No More Excuses

Tell yourself that daydreaming is simply not as exciting or as interesting as actually getting on with building the life you want. Again, begin with awareness and notice the language you use and how you speak about your life. Notice if you often say the following kinds of things to yourself:

> "Ah, I'd love to be a masseuse, but I just don't have any training or anything . . ."
>
> "Wow, I'd love to live in a house like that one day! If only."
>
> "I wish I hadn't given up horse-riding when I was child."

You'll recognize these statements because they are so passive and reactive. If you find yourself saying things like these, stop, slow down, and take a closer look. How can you transform these excuses, daydreams, and regrets into beneficial action *right now*? Maybe you could investigate just exactly what it would take to learn to be a masseuse, or you could look in earnest into how to make your dream home a reality. Maybe you could book to have an outride that very weekend. Often, we speak like this not because we are genuinely out of options, but just because we've convinced ourselves that that's the case. How many anxieties, regrets, fears, and resentments would disappear overnight if people took them out into the light, blew the dust off them, and took concrete action to bring about what they desired?

Create Perspective by Creating Mental Distance

So, we can encourage a relaxed, proactive mindset in ourselves by refusing to let complaining, reactivity, and daydreaming get in the way of what matters most: taking action toward our goals. There is another key way in which a calm and relaxed attitude goes hand in hand with the right psychological perspective—mental "distance."

In the above section on proactiveness, we saw that being able to choose and take control can only actually happen when we are sufficiently aware of what we're doing. If we're lost in emotions, triggered, and stuck in knee-jerk automatic reactions, then we are reactive. To be proactive, we need a little space from that engulfing emotion. We need to take a step back, and from there gain a clear picture of what we're doing, what our options are, and what to do next.

> **Anxious** = trapped or bogged down in strong emotion
>
> **Calm** = able to step above and outside of that emotion

In fact, you could almost say that the degree of anxiety you experience around an issue is directly proportional to how "close" you are to it. Stepping outside of yourself and your emotions for a moment and taking a look at the issue from a distance can not only help you solve the problem, it can make the whole thing seem like less of an emergency! Then, once you're calm, you can take more relaxed, conscious action instead of being reactive.

Great! So how do we create this sense of psychological distance? Does this mean numbing ourselves to our emotions, or getting all cold and clinical about our lives as we look down at everything from the clouds? Thankfully, no!

Introspection Is Not Mind Chatter

Before we go on, it's worth noting what psychological distance *isn't.* Our inner voice can be a great ally, helping us analyze, reflect, weigh options, interpret, remember, and plan. But I probably don't need to tell you that not all self-talk is beneficial. Mental chatter is useless and simply creates more anxiety. You'll know it's mental chatter when:

- It goes round and round in a loop that never stops
- It's often negative/pessimistic
- It prevents you from solving problems rather than helping you
- It makes you feel distracted and disconnected
- It's based in the past or future and not the present
- Most crucially, it increases anxiety while decreasing beneficial action

Reading the above list, you can probably see that the experience of anxiety and the action of negative self-talk are essentially one and the same. Many of us attempt to gain psychological distance only to find we are engaging in more of the same mental chatter that only makes us anxious. So let's now turn to another question—what we are attempting to distance *from.*

Mental chatter, anxiety, and a **loss of conscious awareness** can swallow up our feeling of self-control and agency. The more unaware we are of what is happening to us, the less we are able to take charge of the situation (i.e., we can only be reactive and not proactive). Mental distance is one way we can separate ourselves from strong emotions and the content of our mental chatter so that we can begin to ask, "Wait a second—what *is* this? What am I doing here?"

Without mental distance, we just take our own narratives as gospel and fail to see any way out. On the one hand, we have:

> *Anxiety, narrowing of awareness, loss of agency.*

On the other hand, we have:

> *Calmness, broadening of awareness, control, and responsibility.*

Panic and fear shrink our perspective and rob us of the ability to choose what's best for ourselves, whereas conscious awareness opens our field of view and lets us make healthier choices. Sounds great, but the trouble is, of course, to find a way into that awareness and broadness of vision when you're in the middle of an intense emotion—not easy to do! In fact, you've probably noticed that it's much easier to see other people's blind spots than it is your own. You have distance and perspective; they're too close to see what you can see.

Thankfully, it is possible to learn to create mental distance in ourselves, even in the midst of moments that have us losing our heads.

Kinds of Distance—And How To Create Them

There are many ways to get wrapped up in a strong and engrossing situation. Imagine you are upset after having a fight with your partner. Your body is filled with stress hormones and your heart is pounding, your head is racing with thoughts and you feel chaotic and disorganized, your feelings are all over the place, and all you can focus on is how hurt and alarmed you feel. Okay, now what?

The first type of distance you can help yourself create is **spatial**; i.e., distance in space. This is obvious: You're upset and overwhelmed in your shared home, so leaving the house for a while and taking a walk can give you the shift in perspective you need. But you can also achieve the same result by just changing the room you're in, your proximity to a person, or your bodily position (for example, by standing up if you're slouching). You could simply *imagine* a different location and see how this changes your view on things.

You could also gain **social** distance. This is a more abstract distance between yourself and another person or people. So, even if you stayed with your partner in the same home temporarily, you might find yourself gaining a sense of distance by formally breaking up, for example.

Temporal distance is distance in time. When we're feeling reactive, anxious, or overwhelmed by strong emotions, time seems to stop and we lose the ability to clearly think about the future. But if you can slow down and remind yourself of the future consequences or remember that the present moment is not going to last forever, you give yourself some breathing room in time. In our example, you could actively tell yourself, "I'm upset right now, but I'll sleep on it and I know I'll be thinking more clearly tomorrow morning." This broadens perspective and brings some calm.

Finally, **hypothetical** distance is simply the space we make for ourselves when we imagine that the situation in front of us could possibly be different. This is a big deal. If we can simply acknowledge that there is an option to experience something different than what we're currently experiencing, we are no longer trapped in a moment and can start to think of alternatives, solutions, or creative ways forward. For our example, perhaps you are standing there having a loud shouting match with your partner when you suddenly realize, "Wait. It doesn't *have to* be this way. Maybe I could deal with this argument in a different way than I usually do. Maybe I could calmly remove myself and take a few deep breaths." This puts you straight into a proactive mindset and will dramatically lower your anxiety.

In a way, all distance is created on the back of the realization that the current situation could be different than it is. And you can make it different!

Having perspective on a problem and viewing it from a distance doesn't magically make problems go away or difficult feelings vanish. But it does allow you to temporarily get bigger than those problems, rather than have them overwhelm and swallow you. The problem remains the same, but when you can see it from different angles and retain a degree of awareness, you will instantly feel calmer about it, and with this calm, you can access more options.

Use the Power of Your Imagination To Create Distance

What unfolds in any moment is automatically interpreted by us—we tell a story about it. But we can tell a different story.

If you're in an immediately overwhelming situation (like having a fight with your partner), you may need to quickly create a bit of distance in the moment. But once you've cooled off, you are still left facing the problem. We can defuse strong emotions in the short term, but once the dust settles, we will still need to tackle the underlying problem with patience and focus. In this case, it's worth sitting down and deliberately working through the problem alone, where you can introduce some helpful distance.

A journal is the perfect way to do this. Some people even enjoy talking to a "pet rock" or recording their voice. Sit down where you won't be disturbed for a while and try some of the following techniques.

Advise a Friend

It's easy to see what the best course of action is—when it's somebody else's problem! Take the time to imagine that your problem is actually happening to a close friend of yours and not you. Pull out all your ego and assumptions and resistances and excuses and just look at the plain facts of the story. You might like to write out a brief summary paragraph of the problem as you see it. Then, put little quote marks around the paragraph and literally imagine that those same words were coming from the mouth of someone you care about. What would your response be? How would you advise them?

This seems too simple to work, but it can be useful because we are often impeded from making decisions or acting wisely because denial, fear, or excuses get in the way. We imagine that our problems are super complicated, and we may not notice ourselves ignoring certain features of a situation or twisting others—until we imagine it from someone else's perspective. Sometimes doing this can be relieving in itself because you might suddenly realize your problem isn't as big as you thought it was.

Picture Another Version of Yourself

Granted, the above technique may not always work, and you may genuinely have a complicated case on your hands. If so, try another technique where you imagine what you think of the problem—but from the future. Imagining your future self gives you a different perspective and reminds you that what is happening right now is not what is always going to be happening. Turn your mind to consequences and likely outcomes. After the sting of any strong emotions have worn off, think about what your future self would want.

If you can, think about similar decisions and problems

you've had in the past, but add a temporal element to them. Maybe when you zoom out, you notice that you always do XYZ—and then regret it a few weeks later. By factoring in your future self, you weigh up the present more accurately. At the very least, you can breathe a sigh of relief by simply knowing that the present problem is unlikely to continue unchanged forever.

Reframe Perceptions

During meditation or mindfulness practice, you train yourself to recognize your thoughts as thoughts, and your feelings as feelings. You see them come and you see them go and practice not attaching to them, but merely being aware of their constant flow. You don't need to practice meditation to learn to do this, though. Get into the habit of simply noticing sensations and perceptions.

> "My heart's beating really fast right now."
>
> "I feel disappointed that she said that."
>
> "I'm scared and I hate what's happening."

Importantly, just notice these things, without arguing, interpreting, analyzing, praising, or judging them. You don't have to "accept" them, either; just see that they're there, and that's that. Once you do, you can start to see that it's your choice how you frame and interpret those neutral sensations. For example:

> My heart is beating fast > I must be nervous > I shouldn't be nervous; I've done this a thousand

> times before > If I'm nervous, there's something wrong with me > And so on.

If you notice this happening, you can intercept the situation and experiment with reframing the sensations in different ways, thus creating some distance and bringing a calmer perspective on things.

Perhaps your heart is beating fast because you're doing something new and exciting? Perhaps your heart is beating fast because you're human and doing something a little nerve-wracking, and it's all perfectly okay? Getting this distance, however, requires we first slow down, notice what we're doing, and then notice the places where we can make different choices.

Takeaways

- The biggest difference between those who are anxious and those who aren't might be the difference between being *proactive* and *reactive*. To be proactive is to hold the perspective that you are in charge of and responsible for your life, and create conditions as you will them rather than react to conditions created by others.
- There are many ways to make this mindset shift. Firstly, commit to dropping blaming others or complaining about situations without taking action. If you notice yourself passively whining or resenting others, ask, "*What action can I personally take to change my situation?*"

- Change and difficulty is inevitable, but we can practice being flexible, creative, and solution-oriented rather than getting bogged down by things not going our way. This reduces anxiety.
- We can be more proactive when we stop daydreaming or thinking about "one day" or "if only"—again, we can take inspired action, right now, to empower ourselves.
- To gain a calm, proactive mindset, we can practice putting some distance between us and any strong emotions or thoughts we have. With psychological distance, we gain a broader perspective and empower ourselves to become conscious of our thoughts as thoughts, thus making space to choose consciously and proactively. By creating spatial, temporal, or hypothetical distance, we are no longer at the mercy of external events, but have an internal locus of control.
- Our imaginations can also help us gain much-needed distance and clarity. You can imagine yourself advising a friend to see a fresh perspective on an issue. You can also visualize another version of yourself to entertain other possibilities and alternatives. Finally, you can practice reframing perceptions and notice how you think and feel without attaching any stories, value judgments, or resistance to that awareness. This alone brings calm, but also opens up a space for a new perspective to emerge.

CHAPTER 2

Stepping off the Carousel

Your Anti-Anxiety Superweapon: Going Meta

In the last chapter, we saw how the creation of distance allows you to try on different, potentially better perspectives and witness your own physiological, mental, and psychological processes as an observer, rather than as an unconscious participant tangled up in it all. This kind of detachment may have reminded you of another popular approach to mental health issues of all kinds: meditation and mindfulness practice.

Can mindfulness help you cultivate a sense of calm in your life? Absolutely. However, "mindfulness" can mean so many things. In this chapter, we'll explore a mindfulness-based technique especially helpful for managing emotions and bringing a sense of calm control to your life. It's called ACT: acceptance and commitment therapy.

The acronym simply speaks to the two parts of the approach:

- We **accept** what we cannot control.
- We **commit** to taking action with the things we can in order to better our lives.

Both acceptance and commitment to action allow you to proactively manage your thoughts and emotions—your lived experience. They are skills that have mindfulness at their core, and they work in tandem to help you create the life you want; i.e., the life that aligns with the things that matter the most to you and your values.

In ACT, mindfulness is about being open, aware, and focused on the present. We approach our work with our "observing self"; i.e., the part of us that is aware of everything that is unfolding in the moment. This is the meta position we spoke about, which allows for distance and perspective. Unlike meditation, however, the mindfulness in ACT is more of a set of skills, and something we connect to the concrete world through conscious action.

We can use ACT techniques on the spur of the moment throughout our day, or we can practice more deliberately in the longer term with a therapist—or both. They are simple, however, and can be mastered on your own—all you need is to activate your conscious "observing self." The goal of ACT, however, is not exactly to make you calm; rather, in time, you learn how to increase your psychological flexibility. This means your observing self is strengthened and you are better able to stay in the present and take action according to your values, increasing your quality of life. Problems don't magically disappear—but you become more resilient, more responsive, and more masterful at how you deal with them.

Does having this transcendent, meta, observing self mean you are permanently detached from life and your own emotions? Actually, it's the opposite! From the ACT perspective, anxiety and unhappiness often come from "experiential avoidance", which is the inner resistance toward unwanted thoughts, feelings, and sensations. Avoiding your experience in the present may work temporarily but fails in the long term and creates psychological suffering. The paradox is that by gaining some distance from strong sensations, thoughts, and emotions in the moment, we are actually able to see them, accept them, and work with them by taking action. In this way, we engage *more* with life. According to this approach, then, mindfulness is not used to stay lofty and removed from experience, but to bring you into healthy and sustainable conscious contact with the present moment and everything you experience in it.

In ACT, there are six "core processes" that you can think of as tools in a toolkit to help you manage life and build psychological flexibility. The processes do overlap. Let's consider each with a real-life example (and it always does come down to real life!).

Contacting the Present

Sounds serious, but this is simply being aware and conscious in your observing self, rather than being mindlessly carried by sensations or being trapped inside experiences (i.e., reactive). Here we have full, real awareness in the here and now. We are receptive, alive, and alert. In ACT, all you have is the present—the future hasn't arrived, and the past is long gone. All our power to engage with life and make choices rests right here in the present, so that's where we focus!

Even if you're not into meditation at all, you can gain a lot by practicing grounding techniques that bring you to the present via your senses. Your mind can race around to the future or the past, or frighten itself with hypothetical stories and possibilities. Your body, however, can only ever be in one place: the present. So, when you connect with your body, you necessarily connect with the present. Your body is your anchor—or rather, you have five anchors: sight, sound, smell, taste, and touch.

You can practice grounding techniques any time you like, whether it's to get out of an anxiety spiral or simply as a well-being practice akin to exercise or eating your veggies. Try the 5-4-3-2-1 technique, where you pause to sink into five things you can see, then four things you can hear, three you can touch, two you can smell, and one you can taste. The exact details are unimportant. All that matters is that you completely immerse yourself in the present moment using your senses. You automatically take yourself away from anxious rumination, give yourself distance, and become able to see thoughts and feelings for what they are.

As an example, imagine the doctor has just diagnosed you with Stage 3 cancer. You feel like you've been hit by a bus. The first tool you take out the toolkit is to simply *become aware that you are having an experience.* You might sit down and go into your observing self by noticing your bodily reactions, your initial thoughts, and your feelings. You take a deep breath. You just look at the moment around you and take it in.

Cognitive Defusion

This is where we step back and detach. In ACT, we learn to see our perceptions and thoughts for what they are: images, symbols, bits of information, stories, memories, and assumptions. What they are *not*: absolute reality, laws, or something that has complete control over us.

Let's quickly explore what is meant by cognitive fusion. When we act as though our thoughts are the same as reality, we can say that we are fusing the two. We believe that what we think is precisely the same as what is actually happening, one hundred percent true, and of total importance. Sometimes, in fused thinking, we assume that our thoughts need to be obeyed, or that they're orders. We think that our knee-jerk assumption is wise or all-knowing.

The truth is, however, that there is a difference between our symbol of a thing and the thing itself. When we become aware that our thought about a situation and the situation are two different things, we defuse. We realize that we are using language to tell ourselves a story that we then believe unquestioningly. Defusing is not forcefully imagining the world in a way that it isn't; rather, it is us undoing the process of fusing our thoughts with reality. In the same way as the word "apple" is not an apple, our idea of a situation is not the situation.

In our example, we could get caught up in extreme anxiety and sadness, and tangled up in hopelessness or despair or anger. But if we contact the present and then go still inside ourselves, we can gain perspective. We can be *outside* our experiences, rather than tumbled along *inside* them. This could be as simple as saying, "I'm feeling a lot of confusion right now," instead of "What the hell am I going to do?"

Acceptance

This is *not* condoning or agreeing with what we find in the present moment. It is simply acknowledging that what is happening is, in fact, happening. We don't resist it, argue with it, pretend it doesn't exist. We simply give it room to be what it is. Accepting something doesn't mean we necessarily like it or understand it, only that we openly and plainly agree that it is our reality.

A more helpful term may be "expansion." We simply make room for what is. Imagine you are simply becoming aware of what is happening, as though you were an alien who had never experienced that thing before and had no memories, expectations, assumptions, or fears—you just observed what you observed. Some ACT practitioners advice "breathing into" a sensation. Maybe you notice that there's a tight feeling across your chest. How could you make room for, and breathe into, this sensation?

Instead of interpreting it ("you're stressed"), resisting it ("oh, it's nothing"), or getting panicked ("is there something wrong with my heart?"), you just make room. You notice the sensation, the temperature, the various feelings and where they occur, and how. You breathe into this awareness, expanding into it.

In our example, we might be tempted to think, "Get a grip, you're being too dramatic about all this," or "Chin up," or even "Why aren't you more upset? You must be in denial. You're not doing this right . . ."

Instead, we could simply accept how we are, as we are, without needing to rush along to a conclusion or fix anything or escape uncomfortable sensations. Actually, when you stop struggling against sensations this way, you often allow them to move on, and they have less impact on you, not more.

The Observing Self

There is a part of you that is in the world, experiencing. There is also a part of you that is outside it, unchanging, non-judgmental, aware, unable to be harmed—we call it the observing self. Experience and change wash over us, but there is a part of us that is always there, unaffected. When we are in our observing self, we are detached enough to know that no experience will last forever, control us, or be dangerous to us. Our observing self is curious, open, and interested in life, and never resists or avoids it. This self can see all without being flooded by it. No matter what we experience or how intense it is, there is always some part of us set aside that is unaffected and able to observe while disidentified. It's this self that gives us the power of choice. It's this self that lets us identify our values and choose actions toward those values—regardless of the fleeting experiences we have.

Here, it's important to distinguish between your awareness and your ordinary mental cognitive processes. Being aware is not the same as simply thinking. In thinking, we generate ideas, delve into memories, engage our beliefs, and so on . . . but when we are aware, we simply *observe* what the thinking mind creates. In thinking, we might believe, "I'm unhappy, things shouldn't be as they are," but in our observing self, we merely note, "This is how things are." Those who struggle with anxiety can often find mindfulness doesn't help precisely because they have mistaken everyday rumination for being "aware."

In our example, the observing self is able to take a step back from the experiencing self—in effect, there are two selves. One is having a shocking, painful experience, while the other is observing that shock and that pain. "My head seems to be all over the place right now. My body is suddenly all tense and I feel like I could cry. I've had some bad news and am obviously having a strong reaction . . ."

Find Your Values

Awareness in itself is extremely valuable. But the power of ACT is that we can become aware, and then put that awareness into a bigger context.

> What actually matters to us?
>
> What do we care about most?
>
> What kind of people do we want to be?
>
> Why are we here on this planet?
>
> What are we most prepared to stand for, create, or defend?
>
> What brings purpose, joy, and meaning to your life?

We say that ACT helps us create a better life, but it's our own unique personal values that help us decide what that "better" actually looks like. In your heart, you have certain principles and cherished beliefs that help you orient yourself so that you feel you are living with integrity and purpose. Goals are shorter term and singular. Values, however, speak to our bigger-picture direction in life.

Sometimes, values will be in conflict, or unclear, or even change. That's okay. You can keep asking, "What are my values right now, right here, with regard to this situation?" If you ask yourself often, you will never wander too far!

Returning to our example, with time, we might be able to consciously say to ourselves, "I am a person who has never wanted to be guided or controlled by fear. I'm a brave person and I value courage. No matter what happens to me with respect to my health, I know that I can always choose to be strong and dignified, and that itself gives me courage."

Take Committed Action

Finally, when your values are clarified and you are aware of them, you can engage in the final process: committed action. No, this is not just any old action, but valued action. Action without conscious inspiration or purpose is useless at best and harmful at worst. However, you can act at any moment if you have enough conscious awareness to be guided by your values. But it's up to you to give your actions shape and meaning.

Perhaps you decide that you're going to find out as much information about your cancer diagnosis as possible, keep informed and proactive, and take responsibility for your own health rather than allowing fear and panic to take over. Perhaps you keep a journal and note some questions to discuss with your doctor or make a conscious choice about how you're going to speak to your family about your diagnosis.

As you can see, the ACT approach combines awareness and acceptance and uses it to initiate conscious, value-driven action that actually makes your life better. You change your relationship to your inner experience and to life itself. You give yourself more control and reduce the influence that external events have on you. When you cannot change circumstances, the acceptance part allows you to come to terms with it. When you can change your circumstances, you do so from an empowered, aware position and make sure that your actions reflect what ultimately matters in your life. Think of it as a way to make mindfulness more applicable and practical in everyday life—as well as more personally meaningful.

Now, all of the above may seem like a lot to remember! But there is a simple way to bring the ACT approach into your life right now:

Remember the **ACT** acronym.

> **A** – **Accept** your internal experience in the present moment.
>
> C – **Choose a valued direction**.
>
> **T** – **Take action** in that direction.

For example:

> A – Accept. Notice that you are feeling sad and excluded by friends who've uninvited you from their event. Accept, expand, and breathe into these feelings from your observing self, without judgment or avoidance.
>
> C – Choose a valued direction. Remember that you value kindness and compassion in your relationships. Choose to forgive and forget while being kind to yourself and knowing that you have innate value, whether your friends recognize it or not.

T – Take action. Call up another friend or do something else you enjoy instead rather than dwelling on the feelings of rejection.

Getting the Upper Hand on Rumination

In the next chapter, we are going to look more closely at the content of anxious thoughts and how we can tease apart those thoughts and rewrite them so they work better for us. For now, however, let's simply become aware of the phenomenon of overthinking in itself; i.e., rumination. Rumination and worry go hand in hand. In fact, you can think of rumination as an anxiety-creating engine!

Ordinarily, your brain is a marvelous tool that helps you solve problems, create new things, and identify goals to work toward. Thinking is *wonderful*. It's what allowed your ancestors to learn, avoid danger, and correctly appraise their environment. However, the same mental process can become a nightmare if it spirals out of control. As they say, the mind is a good servant, but a terrible master.

How Do You Identify Rumination?

Going over details again and again, working ourselves into a froth, obsessing over possibilities, getting down on ourselves, trying to stop thinking but being unable to, or rehearsing imaginary scenarios or discussions . . . all of these are part of ruminating. Our brain thinks it's helping, but it's just chewing on things over and over until you're a stressed-out mess. What's the difference between ordinary thinking and ruminating? That's easy: Normal thinking helps us solve problems and learn. Rumination is useless—all it does it make us feel bad.

The truth is that we all ruminate at times. We all get caught up in irresistible thoughts. But we can choose how to respond to those thoughts. Let's stay in a proactive, open, and curious mindset and look at *why* we might ruminate. Usually, it's one of two things we're trying to do:

- Prepare for the future
- Learn from the past

Research shows that we actually do feel *temporarily* less stressed when we're worrying and ruminating over something. Worry, then, can give us the illusion of control—we imagine that the more we worry, the better prepared we are for a future scenario, or the more thoroughly we have processed a past one. But the relief is an illusion, and short-lived. That's because it doesn't really serve any purpose.

A big sign that you're ruminating rather than just thinking is that you're going around in circles. Normal thinking has a start and an end, whereas rumination seems to cover the same ground over and over. It doesn't ultimately help, and it doesn't yield any fresh insights; i.e., you don't learn anything new.

One tell-tale sign of rumination is its emotional charge. Focusing on a worst-case scenario and all the gruesome details? You're probably ruminating. True, the worst thing might happen, but if you catch yourself focusing on exclusively the worst things that can happen and ignoring any potentially good or neutral outcomes, you are likely ruminating.

Why You Shouldn't Challenge Your Thoughts

A common technique (in CBT (cognitive behavioral therapy), for example) is to challenge thoughts that arise and try to replace them with more accurate ones. The trouble is, though this intellectually sounds right, it seldom works.

Remember "experiential avoidance"? When you argue with yourself, you are essentially disagreeing with your current reality and adopting a judgmental, intolerant attitude to what is.

You cannot help what automatically and spontaneously emerges in your mind. So what good will it do to argue or fight against it with *more ideas* about what you *should* think instead? In fact, this process more often spells the beginning of an anxiety and rumination spiral rather than the end to one.

Yes, our thoughts are information and symbols and stories only. They are not necessarily truth. But if we can adopt a mindset of curious and compassionate investigation, we can be aware of all this without judging or forcefully pushing ourselves to think something else. At the very least, sometimes it's not possible to argue with yourself over what the "right" thought is. You often don't know! If you're dealing with unknowns, it's not helpful to try and talk yourself into the thought you think you should be having.

Rather, try to practice discernment. There is no need to challenge or argue with yourself. It's not a war. Instead, be soft, gentle, and curious, and ask yourself:

Is this thought helping me in any way?

By helpful, we mean we want to know if it's going to lead us where we want to go. Note that we are not asking whether a thought is true or good. It's not a moral judgment. This is because a thought can be true but still very, very unhelpful. Dwelling on it may be a bad idea even if it is one hundred percent accurate. So many of us get caught up in overthinking because we are making judgments about good and bad, and maybe even beating ourselves up in the process. But this is not a useful metric.

But it's easier to shift to a question of helpful versus unhelpful. This brings things down to earth and puts them in the context of your life and what you're trying to achieve. Just like we did when we considered ACT, we use action as a yardstick. A thought can be said to be helpful if, in having it, we are more inspired to act according to our values. If a thought encourages us, makes us more resilient, gives us ideas for future plans, helps us cope, or teaches us something, it's helpful. We basically want to take a thought, hold it up to the light, and ask, "*What does this actually create for me?*"

Some examples will make the point clear.

Here's a thought: "My relationship is making me unhappy." If you think this thought, what are the results? You'll be unhappy, and your attention and focus will be drawn to this unhappiness. And that's about it. The thought is true, but thinking it doesn't really . . . go anywhere. If you are guided by this thought, the most likely scenario is that you will just sit with those feelings of unhappiness. You'll feel frustrated and passive.

You could also think, "Everything's fine; there's nothing to worry about," and in this case, the thought will be untrue and unhelpful! Guided by this thought, you stick your head in the sand and stay in a relationship that isn't working.

Finally, you could think, "I don't seem to want to be in this relationship anymore, but I haven't made any choice yet. I seem to be afraid of making the decision." This thought is different. It acknowledges the unhappiness but makes room to solve the problem and take action. This one is a lot more *useful* than the other two, because if you're guided by this one, you are more likely to take action and come to a resolution.

Ruminating thoughts seem helpful, but on closer examination are not. They don't give you any practical information, suggest a path forward, or hint at a solution. If you can start looking at your thoughts in terms of their actionable value, you'll be able to gain perspective, be more proactive, and use thinking as a tool rather than a pointless exercise in stressing yourself out.

Well, what if you can't think of any solutions? This is tricky, but the answer is obvious: If thinking doesn't and can't help your problem . . . then don't think about it! You might be too upset or emotional to see a solution at that moment, or you might need to be patient and wait for the situation to evolve a little. Either way, rumination won't help and may, in fact, muddy the waters further. In this case, find a healthy distraction. Come back to the problem later and look at it with fresh eyes. This is not the same as avoidance; you are consciously acknowledging that a problem needs solving, but you are also recognizing that you're not in a state of mind to find the solution just yet.

Returning to ACT from the previous section, you might notice yourself being completely overwhelmed and upset and choose to say to yourself, "I'm not getting anywhere here. I'm going to stop, take a breather, and go for a long run until my head clears." This can be enough to calm you down and get you into a frame of mind where rumination won't take over.

Your brain is like a powerful problem-solving machine. Thinking is what it does. But ultimately, it's you (your conscious awareness and intention) who is in charge. If you are obsessed with worrying about a problem that *cannot* be solved, then it is up to you to turn the brain machine off, or redirect it. Without anything to stop it, your brain will furiously try to solve an unsolvable problem. But you can always connect with that bigger part of yourself, with your observing self, and choose to drop rumination that isn't helping you. Here, acceptance comes into play. This may mean consciously choosing to acknowledge and even embrace a situation that isn't great, but can't be changed. We have to be in charge of our brains and say, "Thanks, brain, but your problem-solving skills are no longer needed."

Remember that there is no need to challenge your thoughts or do battle with them. You don't need to try and stop those thoughts. Instead, know that as a human being, all kinds of thoughts will pop up in your mind—helpful and unhelpful, true and untrue. But all they are is thoughts. You can always be aware of them, notice what is happening, and choose for yourself what to do with them once they've popped up.

A helpful thought can guide you, inspire you, help you see a solution, or bring you a learning insight.

An unhelpful one keeps you stuck in a loop. It constricts your awareness and keeps you in a strange tunnel of your own creation. Inside that tunnel, we miss out on important information!

However, being calm, collected, and in control doesn't mean having clean, pristine minds with only "good" thoughts coming up. Instead, we will have all the same thoughts and ideas as normal, but we will now be outside this cycle, able to watch it from afar and consciously choose whether any of those thoughts work for us and our values. What freedom it is to know that having a thought doesn't *mean* anything—it's just a thought!

The way off the carousel of rumination and overthinking is simply to get into that observing self and realize that we can decide what's important. We can sift through those thoughts and pick out what's useful and drop what's not useful. We can choose how to act—or whether to act at all. Our conscious awareness and action are where our power lies—our thoughts are not able to control or trap us.

Strategies for Empowerment

The thought doesn't matter. What you *do* with the thought matters.

Once identified, unhelpful ruminations can be reframed into actions that bring value and help to your life. Remember, when we are cognitively "fused," we believe that our thoughts are all-powerful, ruling over us as Absolute Undeniable Truth that we have to obey. But that's an illusion, and it's really we who are in charge. Once you realize this, it's easy to get off the rumination carousel and find that deep, still calm within yourself. Here are a few ways to switch your mindset and remind yourself of your power.

Understand the Root of Your Rumination

An ongoing rumination habit serves some purpose—what is it? What psychological need does it fill? Typically, rumination feels like problem solving, and it feels like being in control. Sometimes, we revert to this bad habit when we feel helpless or vulnerable. Other times, we overthink because we believe it will reduce the anxiety of uncertainty. For some people, overthinking is simply a way to stay mentally entertained or feel superior to others. Whatever it is, if you can pinpoint the role rumination plays in your life, you can take steps to meet that need more usefully (there's that word again!). You may need to find ways to learn to tolerate uncertainty and the discomfort of not always being in control.

You might think that relinquishing control is quite scary, but the truth is that having a little faith, trusting in others, or simply accepting things that you cannot know or control can actually make you feel less anxious overall. You can build your tolerance by slowly giving up control to others (more often than not, this is just the illusion of control anyway!).

Practice Kind Compassion and Forgiveness

Maybe you often ruminate on past wrongs, arguments, bad feelings, and so on. You can't forgive or forget, and you play over bad scenes from your life, either blaming yourself or getting bitter by blaming others. In this case, forgiveness and compassion is the only cure. Many people fail to forgive because they misunderstand what it is: Forgiveness is something you do not for others, but for yourself. It doesn't make the pain go away or undo the past. What it does is consciously allow you to release that and move on from it. Forgiving someone or yourself doesn't mean you forget, and it doesn't mean you condone or agree with what happened. It doesn't mean you are okay with what is wrong or that you want to ignore or downplay injustice. It simply means you are consciously choosing to put your attention where it can help you. Forgiveness has nothing to do with other people; it's a quiet decision we make within ourselves to let go and say that we don't need anyone's permission or "closure."

The 3M Strategy

Finally, there is one very concrete and practical way to pull yourself out of anxious rumination in the moment. It's called the 3 M's:

Move.

Make.

Meet.

Sometimes, you just need something short and swift to kick you out of a downward thought spiral and get you into a state of mind where you can start choosing more consciously again.

First, see if you can move. Change gear and get out of your head, and engage in a little healthy physical distraction. Hit the gym, go for a long walk, or dance around your kitchen for a few minutes.

You could also make something. Rumination is characterized by impotent, useless mental activity that achieves nothing. Counteract this by delving into creative and useful activity; i.e., make something. It doesn't matter what it is; just take action to bring something new into the world instead of living in your head. Bake a cake. Do some housework or try some home DIY. Paint a picture, repair a broken pair of shoes, crochet a doily, or organize your spice cupboard.

Finally, you could try meeting up with someone. Rumination is very internal and private, and it gets carried away precisely because it isn't regulated and kept in check by the outside environment. Social connection can help ground you and give you perspective, as well as slow you down and get you feeling happy and recharged. This can be an extremely effective way of getting unstuck from your own thought spirals.

The 4 A's of Stress Management

This is tangentially similar to the previous point of moving, making, or meeting. This technique can be like a lifeboat in the storm of stress and overthinking. It's easier to get into than meditation and will help you quickly get a handle on everyday life stressors. All you need to remember is four techniques: **avoid**, **alter**, **accept**, and **adapt**. It can be a comfort in itself to know that there are really only these four possible ways to respond to any life stress. If you can, write them down somewhere you can see it at a glance until you've drilled it into your mind and can remember it instantly.

The first thing you can do is **avoid**.

It sounds suspiciously simple, but there's a lot of aggravation in life you can simply walk away from. We can't control everything in life, but we can arrange our circumstances so that we don't have to be in stressful surroundings or with stressful people. If we're honest, we might see that a lot of the stress in our lives is voluntary—and we don't have to agree to it!

Think about what is stressing you in your environment and how you can take control to moderate or remove it entirely. Consider someone who hates how busy the grocery stores are on Saturday mornings. Knowing that this stresses them out, they can rearrange their schedule so they do their weekly shopping at the quietest time—say, on Tuesday evenings. There's no need to manage the stress of a busy supermarket if you just avoid it entirely.

You can avoid stressful people in exactly the same way. Do you find that your stress goes through the roof when your parents come to stay for the holidays? Find a way to have them stay in a nearby B&B, or avoid planning any activities where you are all alone together in a room for hours with nothing to do but stress each other out.

When you avoid stress, you are not running away from obligations or denying genuine problems. You are simply learning to say "no" to stress that is unnecessary and harmful. We can always say no to situations and people that demand too much of us and our resources. Those resources can be mental energy and attention, but they can also be time. If something in your life is gobbling up all your time, you *can* say no.

Look at your to-do list and get rid of two or three items that are not urgent and not priorities. Delegate tasks, or let someone else take on a responsibility. You don't have to do it all! So, the next time you face a stressful prospect, ask yourself, "Can I just avoid this whole thing?" If you can, do so. This is not only a big step toward creating healthy boundaries, it's a way of simplifying and streamlining life and getting in touch with your guiding values. So much of our anxiety and stress comes from areas of life we don't even care about, if we're honest. Why waste your sense of balance and well-being on something that doesn't ultimately matter or mean anything to you?

If you can't avoid the situation, you might need to find ways to change it; i.e., **alter** it.

You always have the option of asking others to change their behavior. For example, if the builders are making a racket outside, politely ask them to pause for ten minutes while you finish an important phone call. Communicate your needs and feelings directly, rather than suffering in silence. If you never clearly tell your friend that his stupid jokes really hurt you, you may sit quietly and bear the brunt of it forever, when it would have been easy to tell him how you feel and ask him to stop.

We can't avoid every stress in life, but we often have a say in how these events unfold. Talk to people, negotiate, and use "I" statements to share your needs and ask for what you want. If you can't help but go to the store on a Saturday morning, play an audiobook on your phone and listen to it while you shop, if that relaxes you. If you can't avoid that extra PTA meeting, try to lump it in with other errands you're already doing so you save time, effort, and potentially gas for your car. You can also do a lot to alter unavoidable situations by cutting them down to a more manageable size. If you can't get out of going to that boring party, go but be upfront in the beginning and say, "Unfortunately, I have to go in an hour—early start tomorrow!"

In meditation, we watch stressful and anxious thoughts as they arise and consciously choose our response to them. But with careful avoidance and management, we can actually step in and tweak our lives so that stressful thoughts don't get as much chance to appear in the first place. We can engineer a lifestyle that is in itself minimally stressful—or at least make sure that what stress remains is genuinely worth it.

Basically, if you can't avoid a stressor, ask what you can do to change it.

If your answer is "not much," then you might need to go one step further and **accept** it.

How do you accept a situation you dislike? First, if you dislike it, then you dislike it. Acceptance doesn't mean pretending you don't feel how you feel; it's an acknowledgment that it's *okay* to feel that way. Validate your own emotions and own them. For example, your boyfriend has just broken up with you via text, and there's not much you can do about his decision. But you can work on accepting the situation by calling up a friend to share your feelings.

If the situation is one in which you've been wronged, acceptance may take the form of trying to find a way to forgive. Remember that forgiveness is something you do for yourself and not the other person. When you forgive, you are releasing yourself from the stress and energy of resenting and blaming the other person.

Acceptance may also be about the subtle shifts in the way we frame events. We can't change the events themselves, but we can watch how we talk about them inwardly and the language we use. For example, instead of saying, "I completely failed my course and wasted my money. I'm such an idiot for not working harder," you could say, "I made a mistake and I'm not happy about it. But this one event doesn't define me. I can learn from mistakes and move on. I can do better next time."

Acceptance doesn't mean we agree with what happened or that we like it and shouldn't try to change it. It only means we gracefully come to terms with what we can't realistically change so we can focus on what we can. This step can be a powerful tool for overcoming the kind of anxiety that comes with resentment or bitter recollection of things that happened long in the past. Regrets and wishing how things could have, should have, or might have been are a recipe for anxiety. But acceptance diffuses and softens that anxiety and allows you to realize that it cannot be changed.

In the longer term, we do our best in the face of stress if we can **adapt**. Adapting means making more lasting changes to our worldview, our goals, our perception, and our expectations. Picture someone who is a perfectionist and is always stressed out because they never seem to meet their high standards. The best approach isn't that they find a way to be Superman, but instead lower their expectations so they're more reasonable and in line with reality. They have not magically found a way to completely overhaul their reality, but instead have adapted to that reality and evolved into a form that's better suited to it.

Adapting to stress means we change *ourselves* to better cope with life. You might simply refuse to engage in depressing thoughts and deliberately practice being a person who is more optimistic. When we alter our perspective, we can see things differently. Is this a "crisis" or a "challenge"? How does this obstacle look when we tell ourselves, "I'm a resilient person," compared to when we tell ourselves, "Life isn't fair. This will end badly like everything does."?

When we adapt to stress, we find ways to make ourselves stronger. We build a worldview for ourselves that empowers us. For example, someone might get into the habit of making a "gratitude list" every day of all the wonderful things they are actually blessed with in life. Another person might meditate on their own personal "code" or say a mantra daily to remind them that they are strong and they can get through adversity. If we have an arsenal of powerful attitudes, ideas, philosophies, and inspiration, we can go into the world knowing that we can handle stress—and maybe even be better people for it!

With time, practicing meditation can achieve some of these core-level changes and genuinely alter how we see ourselves and the world. But any time we are actively and consciously engaging with meaning, we are building our own characters and our own vision of who we are as people. You might see yourself today as someone who is hounded by anxiety. But there is also strength in realizing that you have other amazing qualities, too—diligence, kindness, intelligence, creativity, humor. And all of these can help you frame and offset your anxiety.

So, those are the 4 A's of stress management. When you find yourself feeling anxious, pause and run through each of them in sequence. No matter how stressful the situation, there is a way for you to engage with it mindfully and proactively. You are not helpless in the face of stress—you have tools at your disposal! To use these tools, all it takes is a little awareness.

For example, there may be a colleague at work who stresses you out daily. Instead of getting overwhelmed by telling yourself there's nothing you can do about it, pause and ask if you can simply *avoid* this colleague. Maybe you can have lunch at a different time to avoid meeting them in the cafeteria, or maybe you can physically move to work farther away from them. But let's say you can't avoid encountering them in weekly meetings, and this is where they frequently interrupt you or steal your ideas.

You think of ways to *alter* the situation. Can you get out of these meetings? Can you speak to your colleague privately and share your concerns ("I'm uncomfortable in meetings lately, and I feel dismissed when you interrupt me")? Can you speak up in meetings and assert stronger boundaries when you talk? If none of these are really possible, you can still *accept* the situation to some degree. You might confide in a close friend about your frustrations, or come to realize that this colleague actually interrupts everyone, so you won't continue to take it personally or let it stress you.

Finally, you can adapt by working on becoming an overall more confident and assertive person. When you genuinely feel that you have as much right to speak as anyone else, then you may feel more confident saying, "Sorry, I was still speaking," and carrying on calmly. Instead of stewing over what you *should* have said that evening, you have simply said it and moved on.

Takeaways

- When it comes to anxiety, rumination, and overthinking, mindfulness practices can help if they are tethered to concrete action in the moment, as outlined in the ACT model. In acceptance and commitment therapy, we accept what we cannot control and commit to taking action to change the things we can according to our personal values in order to improve our lives.
- In ACT, anxiety is often about experiential avoidance, which we can counteract using the six core principles.
- The first is to genuinely contact the present without judgment, interpretation, resistance, or narrative, but with conscious alertness and open curiosity about what is unfolding in the now.
- The second is cognitive defusion, where we separate out our thoughts about reality from reality itself. We accept our thoughts as thoughts so we don't get tangled up in them. The third is acceptance, where we welcome and acknowledge reality without arguing with it. We don't have to agree or condone, only observe. We use the fourth

concept, the observing self, to have a conscious "meta" perspective on our thoughts. One part is having an experience, while another part is observing us having that experience.

- The fifth is to find our values and principles so that we can put our thoughts into context. The observing self can appraise our thoughts and compare them against our values so we can do the sixth principle—take conscious, inspired action.
- The acronym ACT can help us: Accept your internal experience in the present moment, choose a valued direction, and take action in that direction. This reduces anxiety and overthinking.
- Overcoming anxious rumination is about learning to identify it. Compared to normal cognition, rumination is endless, doesn't bring insight, and doesn't actually improve anything, even though it temporarily feels like problem-solving.
- "Challenging your thoughts" isn't necessary and only plays into further experiential avoidance and resistance. Instead, ask if a thought is useful and whether it's helping you achieve goals in accordance with your values. Compassion, forgiveness, and the 3M strategy (meet, make, move) are also great strategies for empowering yourself out of rumination.
- There is a mantra called the 4 A's of stress management. These are avoid, alter, accept, and adapt. Avoiding things entails simply walking

away from things you can't control. Some things are just not worth the effort and are best removed from our environments altogether. However, if we can't avoid it, we must learn how to alter our environment to remove the stressor. If we can't alter our environment, we have no choice but to accept it. Lastly, if we can't do much about the situation at all, we must adapt to it and learn how to cope with our stressor and reduce its damaging potential to a minimum.

CHAPTER 3

The Art of Cognitive Restructuring

How To Reframe Automatic Negative Thoughts

In the last chapter, we tried to shift our focus onto all the ways we can inhabit our observing self or higher conscious awareness and saw how this allows us to observe our experience, notice when we're ruminating, and choose to step in and act according to our values. We said that "challenging" your thoughts doesn't usually work because it can be a form of "experiential avoidance." In other words, when we push back against what we experience in the moment, we open the door to judgment, self-criticism, and resistance. If our goal is to be more aware, however, we need to drop any attitude of judgment or feeling like certain thoughts are wrong and need to be "challenged."

Instead, we looked at how to *reframe* thoughts according to their usefulness in our particular lives, rather than taking the perspective that certain thoughts or ideas are wrong or bad and need to be corrected. This may seem like a very small distinction to make, but it's important: Approaching any change with an attitude of judgment and negativity is unlikely to work, whereas a proactive, compassionate, and accepting frame of mind will allow us to gently improve without feeling bad about where we currently are. The action we take may be the same in each case, but our intention and attitude behind those actions can make all the difference!

Bringing Awareness to Automatic Thoughts

So, we know that reframing and restructuring thoughts is *not* about "fixing" the wrong thoughts or arguing with your real experience, but about a conscious shift in perspective. When we bring consciousness to what is unconscious, we create choice. So, we are not judging ourselves, identifying problems, and fixing them, but rather shining awareness into the dark corners where there isn't any.

Automatic negative thoughts are an especially "dark corner." Images, beliefs, ideas, and feelings can spring into action in response to a trigger while we're completely on autopilot. Beliefs are really just thoughts we've had for a very long time. Our way of interpreting events may become invisible to us over time and are so reflexive and automatic that we don't question them. While they seem tiny and superficial in the moment, automatic negative thoughts create the fabric of our lived experience and are at the heart of many mental illnesses.

Unchecked automatic negative thoughts create your self-concept and the way you perceive yourself. Without even knowing it, your own cognitive biases shape how you think of the future, what's possible for you, your abilities, and your worth as a human. This impacts *everything* in life, like a filter laid over every single perception, every action, and every story we tell ourselves. Because they're unconscious, automatic negative thoughts can act like a constantly undermining program running in the background of your life, leading to a cycle of negativity that continually reinforces itself.

Most of us don't *think* we are operating in the world with any kind of cognitive bias, but this is precisely the point: The expectations, assumptions, and beliefs that we are not consciously aware of are the most influential in our lives. So, can we just go in and replace all the negative and unhelpful beliefs, then? If you imagine your life is one great tapestry, it's not possible to just remove one stitch without unraveling the entire fabric. In other words, our self-concept and our perspective on the world is complex, and it's not just a matter of replacing a single thought as though it were a faulty circuit breaker.

Instead, we can think of the process of transformation as gradual. Superficially challenging thoughts or parroting affirmations is not going to cut it—what we are trying to do is create *a complete shift in perspective* beyond the individual thoughts that emerge.

Let's make all of this concrete with some real-life examples. Picture a teenager who suffers from depression. Their self-concept and life perspective is ultimately pessimistic and manifests as automatic negative thoughts, such as:

> "I'm such a failure."
>
> "I have to do this on my own, and I can't."
>
> "My life is a mess."
>
> "I hate the way I look and the way I am."

These thoughts are a result of a negative orientation to life, but they are also its cause—it's a vicious cycle. Say this teenager takes their driving test one day, for example, but approaches the task with the (automatic, completely unconscious) belief that "Nothing ever works out no matter how hard I try." This affects how they interpret the experience (it's an ordeal and not a fun challenge), how they recuperate from setbacks (hint: they don't), and the actions they take (procrastinating booking the test, taking things personally, and seeing any difficulty as proof that they're a loser . . .).

This teenager could have instead taken their driving test with the deep certainty that they are a good person, that they can learn, that life generally works out okay, and that they are capable of weathering minor setbacks. Even for the exact same driving test, this could completely transform their experience.

Positive automatic thoughts are more along the lines of:

> "Even if something bad happens, I know I'll be okay."
>
> "I can accomplish things if I try hard."
>
> "My life is pretty good."
>
> "I've got a lot of good qualities."

Making any transformation is not simply a matter of replacing a negative thought with a positive one. Remember that automatic thoughts are more of a symptom and manifestation of a deeper set of beliefs and a self-concept. So how do we make *genuine* change?

Cognitive Restructuring

Automatic negative thoughts create damage because we are unaware of them. The first step, then, is to bring **awareness** to our automatic negative thoughts.

> **Step 1:** Identify your cognitive distortions and automatic negative thoughts.
>
> **Step 2:** Rationally and consciously adjust/dispute/engage with these thoughts.
>
> **Step 3:** Put new, more useful thoughts back into the context of your life.

So, for example, someone might be going on a first date. They deliberately practice the principles of ACT and become mindful of what's going on for them. They become conscious of a few themes in their thoughts and notice a recurring thought: "What if they think I'm awful and reject me?" Recognizing that this is a cognitive distortion is step one.

Now, the person can rationally and consciously engage with this thought. Remember, it's not about finding fault or deciding if the thought is true or not. Rather, they ask if it's *useful.* What are the results of this unconscious thought? Well, that's obvious: They don't enjoy the date, they're constantly scanning for signs of rejection, and they're in a reactive, passive state that assigns all choice and agency to the other person while giving up their own. This makes them anxious and, ironically, more likely to behave in a way that people will find unappealing.

For step 2, the person can try to restructure this thought. **What are the alternatives?** Broaden your perspective. Instead of focusing on self-appraisal, why not remember that on a date, *both* people are there to learn more about one another? You could realize that even if your date doesn't like you, it's not the end of the world—not everyone will, right? And besides, there's also a chance that you both really click. And so on.

For step 3, you can take this hypothetical newly adjusted thought and put it to work in your life. Now is the time to use affirmations or to gently nudge yourself toward interpretations or narratives that are closer to what you already consciously know works for you. Whenever you notice the thought "What if they think I'm awful and reject me?" pop up, you have an alternative answer: "What if they don't?" or "So what if they do reject me? They can dislike me, and that wouldn't mean I'm any less lovable a person!"

Will this magically make the date a complete success? No, probably not. But gradually, as you replace the *automatic negative thoughts* with *deliberately positive ones,* you loosen the hold of outdated and unworkable self-concepts and actively choose something that works. Your work is two-fold: You pull what is unconscious and automatic out of the dark and shine the light of awareness on it, and then you give yourself the choice to do something different. You can only make the choice once you are aware of other options, and that's why awareness is the important first step.

Breaking the cycle of negativity isn't something to be done overnight (no matter what motivational speakers or self-help gurus tell you). But the great thing about awareness is that it tends to create more awareness. It's not necessary to pretend to do bland "positive thinking" or get in the habit of contradicting yourself or arguing with your long-held beliefs. Rather, just become curious and open about the thoughts you do hold, shine the light of awareness all over them, find alternatives, and begin to embed those alternative thoughts into your world instead. Stay aware and see what happens.

This takes time and patience—just because a thought is not useful, doesn't mean it will be easy to give up! In fact, you can expect that it will take repeated and consistent practice to start gently shifting your perspective. But it *will* shift with consistent conscious awareness and with the intention to act from awareness rather than from being on autopilot.

Some hints for cognitive restructuring that actually works:

- Practice self-compassion and never approach the task from a position of criticism or judgment, or like a stern drill sergeant who is picking through your brain to find out all the "wrong" thoughts!
- Start, as always, with receptive, curious, and open awareness—don't interpret or condemn; just look and see what is currently happening for you.
- Realize that change takes time—it took you a lifetime to develop your current automatic thoughts and beliefs; be patient as you rework them, and don't expect overnight miracles.
- When you challenge your own thinking, don't take it upon yourself to decide on right and wrong or good and bad. Simply ask what effect your current thoughts are having on your life and whether there may be alternatives that actually fit your values and goals better.
- Forget "positive thinking" and affirmations that work only on the superficial level. You are trying to make a *genuine shift in your perspective*, not just cover your old beliefs in a fresh coat of paint!

Use the Two-Column Technique

Right, let's put this into practice. We want to gain distance from that automatic, mindless, hamster-on-a-wheel mind and see our thoughts for what they are.

A good way to do this is to write things down. On a sheet of paper, draw two columns. On the left, you want to note down some thoughts, ideas, assumptions and beliefs you have become aware of and which you suspect may not be helpful or in alignment with your values.

For example, you might write "I'm never good enough" and "I'm a depressed person."

Take a deep breath and look at these. Take a moment to really *feel* the mindset behind them. Feel how your body responds to these thoughts and ideas. Picture all the times in life you've carried this inner filter over your perspective. Now think of how you behave, how you see yourself, and the stories you tell yourself based on this unconscious and unchallenged belief. Maybe you notice that you shrink and slouch, both literally and figuratively, and hide away in life, never putting your opinion forward, never challenging yourself, and just accepting it when others criticize you.

Just look at all this and notice it. See these thoughts as thoughts—not reality itself, but just pictures, ideas, and symbols in your mind.

Now, in the other column, get creative. How could you rewrite the thought so that it is actually helpful to you? So that it can teach you something or inspire you or help you achieve what you want to achieve? This is not something anyone else can do for you—only you can decide what your values are, and what genuinely inspires you as a "useful" alternative. This is why cut-and-paste affirmations typically don't stick—we haven't taken the time to figure them out for ourselves according to *our* principles and ideals.

Instead of "I'm never good enough," you could write "I'm a normal person with both good and bad qualities," or "When I don't succeed, I learn and work hard to do better next time," or "I love and accept myself even though I'm not perfect." Instead of "I'm a depressed person," you could say, "I'm experiencing some sad feelings at the moment," or "This is a difficult time, but it won't last forever," or even "I am going through some challenging but exciting changes in my life right now." You want to experiment with alternatives that genuinely feel useful and inspiring to you. There's no need to be overly positive or unrealistic, either!

Once you've found some alternatives, don't just write them down. Yes, we rationally disputed/challenged/rewrote these thoughts, but they mean nothing until we absorb them internally and really believe them. So, write them down and take a moment to *feel* how a new thought is different from your automatic one. This is not just an intellectual exercise. How does the alternative thought make you want to behave? How does it feel? How does the world look when you hold this belief? What new solutions or options are now available to you?

There are many great ways to rewrite negative automatic beliefs:

- Replace absolute terms like *always, never, nobody, everything,* etc. with more moderate terms. "I always fail" becomes "I've failed this one time. That doesn't mean I'll fail next time. I have succeeded in the past."

- If your thoughts take on a catastrophizing element, ask yourself if it would really be the end of the world if the worst thing happened. So, "If I fail my exam, it'll be the worst thing that could possibly happen" becomes "I might fail my exam, but even I do, I'll be okay and I still have options."
- For very negative, critical, or self-hating thoughts, just bring in some compassion. Rewrite thoughts as though you were saying them to a loved one. A thought like, "You're a disgusting loser" then becomes "Your behavior wasn't great this time, but it's okay and you'll do better next time."
- Watch for whether you're trying to mind-read, predict the future, or jump to conclusions that are unfounded. Get into scientist mode and ask yourself for evidence. If you write "They'll never agree to give me a raise", you could ask whether you have any evidence to believe this, and if not, rewrite the thought as "I'm worried they may not give me a raise, but I have no reason to think they'll say no, and it's worth asking." The thought "She definitely hates me" becomes "I can't read her mind. I simply don't know her opinion at this time."
- Watch for all-or-nothing or black-and-white thinking and try to see if you're ignoring a third option or missing some crucial information.

> "He hasn't called and I bet he's dead in a ditch somewhere" becomes "He hasn't called, but there could be a number of reasons why."

Finally, one very useful way of rewriting unconscious automatic thoughts is to transform them into useful action. We are always empowered to take worries, concerns, regrets, etc. and rework them into real-world changes. For example, if you have the passive, hopeless thought, "I don't know how to do this," you can rework that into a more empowering thought: "Who can I ask for help?" or "How can I learn to do this?"

"I've made a mistake and I can't bear the consequences" can become "What steps can I take now to mitigate the damage done?" or "What can I do practically to manage the consequences?"

Action is magical—it can get you unstuck, open your mind to possibilities and alternatives, and empower you to feel proactive again. The smaller the better—just identify one positive action you can take in the right direction and watch your perspective shift instantly.

Changing Your World—One Cognitive Distortion at a Time

Once you get the hang of "looking under the hood", cognitively speaking, you may be surprised at just what is lurking there outside your conscious awareness! Your head is bursting with personal myths and narratives, mental schemas, beliefs, assumptions, expectations, and yes, completely weird and irrational thought patterns.

Learning to question and rewrite the building blocks of your inner world can lead to a deep feeling of calm contentment and confidence. It's a wonderful realization: that the way you think *can* be changed. If you practice this in earnest, though, you'll see that it goes deeper than just saying the right words or intellectually grasping what is "rational" and "irrational." It takes courage and honesty to really look and see what your inner world is made of!

In that spirit, let's look more closely at some common negative thought patterns and the way they may appear in your thinking. These are called cognitive distortions. Again, the goal is not to play "gotcha!" with our unconscious minds, but rather to curiously become aware and then challenge ourselves to open up to better alternatives. Chances are, you recognize all of the following:

> **Magnification**—putting all our focus on one aspect or idea, blowing it out of proportion.
>
> Example: "If I don't get the right shoes for my wedding outfit, the entire day is going to be ruined, and I might as well throw my whole marriage out the window."

> **Overgeneralization**—falsely applying one conclusion to other cases in which it doesn't apply.
>
> Example: "In 1992, my girlfriend dumped me for earning less than her, and that's how I know that all women are materialistic gold-diggers."

> **Black-and-white thinking**—lacking shades of nuance in favor of cut-and-dried, oversimplified interpretations.
>
> Example: "He didn't laugh at my joke, so he probably hates my guts."
>
> **Catastrophizing**—focusing on the worst outcome as the most likely.
>
> Example: "They're taking a long time to get my test results back to me . . . I bet I have some rare viral infection that's going to kill me."

There are many other cognitive distortions, but all they all act in the same way: They filter and distort reality and narrow our field of perception. When you practice being more aware, you may notice yourself returning to one or more of these biases again and again.

Technique 1: Socratic Questioning

Cognitive biases are unconscious and unchallenged. Our work is to make them conscious and challenge them! One way to do this is to be curious and ask questions in the style of the famous philosopher Socrates, who used a simple technique to approach truth: the humble question. Here's an example.

> "All women are gold-diggers."
>
> "Really? What evidence do you have?"
>
> "Well, there was Angela back in 1992 . . ."
>
> "Do you have any other evidence?"

> "Well, not *direct* evidence, no. But everyone knows women are like that."
>
> "Is that really true, though? *Everyone*? Is that a thought based on facts, or more on your feelings?"
>
> "Well, I guess it is based a little on my feelings."
>
> "Could you be viewing the situation in absolute terms when a more nuanced approach would be more realistic?"
>
> "Okay, yes, maybe not *all* women are like that. Some are not, that's true . . ."

And so on. Here, you refuse to take your own word for it and question every assumption and expectation. You ask, is this thought *really* true? Why do you think so? Is this rational? Where does this thought come from? Why? What are you *not* looking at? It sounds basic, but the fact is that many of us rush headlong into a belief without taking a second to ask whether we have any evidence for that belief.

Pretend you're an alien with no preferences either way, and just become curious: What do you actually know here? What is fact and what is emotion? Are you making guesses or assumptions or unfounded inferences? Could you be misinterpreting the evidence somehow? Simply become curious about other ways you might interpret the situation and how valid your current position is. Are you sticking to your story simply because you've always done so out of habit? Often, we carry on with a faulty thought because it confirms beliefs and conclusions we already have about ourselves.

Our inner narrative and self-talk can be so persistent that we simply start to accept it. But the Socratic technique is about examining your own validity and perceptions from scratch. You want to encourage yourself to think more broadly, more deeply, and more rationally. In essence, you are using pointed questions to uncover your own biases, blind spots, and faulty logic. You're not merely disagreeing with yourself for the fun of it, but trying to challenge your own lazy or automatic thinking—after all, entertaining other possibilities is the only real way you can start to do things differently!

Technique 2: Guided Imagery

Visualization is a powerful way to focus the mind, direct your attention, and make changes to your thinking. You can buy pre-recorded guided imagery sessions, find them for free online, or make your own. Whatever you decide to do, the idea is that you use your imagination to rehearse or flesh out certain events or images in your mind and thereby practice or rewrite core beliefs on your own terms.

For example, you could identify some alternative thoughts using the two-column exercise above and then take the time to visualize the new thought playing out in real life. You could imagine how a past argument or discussion might play out differently if you approached it from a different perspective, or you could rehearse and upcoming situation from an entirely new point of view. Some people do this daily—they write their morning to-do list and then picture themselves running through the day, imagining in vivid detail how they will cope with various challenges, the words they'll say, and how they will respond to crises.

Use visualization to rehearse or practice a different mindset, or to return to past experiences where you can slow things down and examine what happened, finding the underlying beliefs and looking more closely at them. Alternatively, visualization can simply be a tool to help you sink more deeply into states of minds and emotions that you are trying to cultivate. For example, if you discover that at the heart of much of your rumination is the belief that you are "not enough," then you can use visualization to counteract this. You could imagine past situations where you *did* feel like you were enough. Exploring these images or events, you can allow alternative thoughts to emerge, and expand them. From this point of view, see if you can think of actions to take toward your goals.

There are no limits to your visualization—you could use a guided imagery session to imagine a wise, kind mentor figure encouraging you and giving you advice. You could conjure an inner mental "safe space" where you go to de-stress. You could take the time to imagine in detail a new and idealized form of yourself—what does this person think, feel, do? Allow this to guide you.

Maybe imagine your old self having a conversation with this new self. Or perhaps simply picture images and symbols that have meaning for you. For example, it might be very powerful for you to imagine yourself as a butterfly, transforming in your cocoon, letting go of all your old beliefs, and building new ones for yourself. It's up to you! What's important is that you are not merely rewriting your thoughts on a superficial level, but actually feeling into them. Visualization makes things more real for your brain . . . provided you use all your senses and engage your feelings and sensations.

Technique 3: Keeping a Record or Diary

Writing things down is a natural and easy way to gain distance and perspective, as well as slow your thoughts right down and get a handle on what may seem very abstract. When you are inside your head, identify with your "thought traffic" and allowing your unconscious self-talk to run the show, it's harder to be aware of patterns, distinct ideas, and repeating loops. It's easier, though, if you stop to put things down in black and white.

The two-column technique above is a great way to get a handle on vague thoughts, but there are other ways to use writing to spot and rework cognitive distortions. Think of yourself as a curious scientist whose main goal is simply to understand and document. When something noteworthy happens or you find yourself upset or confused, get out your notebook and write down:

The situation: What's happened? What are the triggers?

Your thoughts: What are you thinking?

Your feelings: What are your emotions and how are they playing out in your body?

Your resulting behaviors: How did you choose to act or respond to these thoughts and feelings? What was the result?

Possible cognitive biases or distortions: Can you identify any recuring patterns, familiar narratives, or plain old irrationality?

Alternative thought: As in the two-column activity, can you identify a different perspective or even a way to convert your thought into concrete action?

What happens when you try the alternative thought: Try to embed the updated thought into your world somehow. How does it feel different? Are you getting different results? Choosing different actions?

As a brief example:

The situation: You've gained ten pounds over Christmas.

Your thoughts: "This is an absolute disaster. You're a total pig and you'll never lose this weight."

Your feelings: Deep shame, self-hate, and a heavy feeling in all your limbs. Wanting to hide away.

Your resulting behaviors: Feel like giving up. Feel like bingeing to feel better!

Possible cognitive biases and distortions: Notice the old pattern of all-or-nothing thinking around body weight, apathy, and catastrophizing. Notice extreme harshness and lack of compassion. No perspective.

Alternative thought: "You've gained weight, but it's not the end of the world. It happens, and I know you're uncomfortable, but with some effort you can lose the weight again." Could ask what can be done to take baby steps toward a solution; i.e., head to the store to stock up on some healthy groceries.

What happens when you try the alternative thought: Don't feel as panicked; don't feel as disgusted with myself. Still feel bad, but now I know there is something I can do to improve the situation. It's easier to act when I don't feel hopeless and self-hating.

When you write things down, you give yourself the chance to notice patterns. Often, just putting things into words give you a sense of control over them. You put your thoughts *out there* on the page and realize that, in fact, that's all they are—words and patterns on a page. They are always just words and patterns in your head! As easily as you can rewrite different words in your notebook, you can shift your inner landscape, too.

Technique 4: Playing with "What If?"

Catastrophizing (and plain old rumination) often have the nagging question of "what if?" at their core. We sit and imagine the worst possible outcome in gruesome detail, then zoom in on it, behaving as though it were not only possible, but likely. Dropping the anxiety around this kind of cognitive distortion is about bringing some sense and reason back into your appraisals. You can do this by switching your perspective on the "what if?" question.

Firstly, catastrophizing is characterized by an illogical focus on only negative outcomes when it's also possible that something good or even great could happen. We ignore all these positive possibilities, and, naturally, the situation starts to look very gloomy indeed. To give yourself a more balanced view, take a piece of paper and draw two columns. On one side, you can note down "negative what ifs", and "positive what ifs" on the other side. Now, the negative might be easier to imagine than the positive, but the power of this exercise is to remind you that a) you actually don't know what will happen and b) you could be pleasantly surprised.

You don't have to force it, but try to come up with an even number of possibilities for each side. Take a look at the list you've created and ask yourself: Is the negative *really* more likely than the positive? Sometimes, deliberately considering the positive potential in a situation gives us a more balanced view on things and dials down anxiety.

Finally, you might do this exercise and realize that, even on closer consideration, there are more negative potential outcomes. Now what?

Positive thinking doesn't mean we live in a world free of negative outcomes, disappointments, or difficult feelings. It's perfectly possible that we will be faced with a situation we dislike—that's life! However, sometimes the most empowered position is to take the approach of asking, "Even if the worst possible outcome came to pass . . . would that really be all that bad?"

Try it. The next time you're catastrophizing, follow the thought to its completion.

> "I'm being sued for malpractice. It's the end of my career, and I'm terrified."
>
> "So? What's the worst that can happen?"
>
> "Well, I lose my job forever! It would be really stressful and devastating."
>
> "Okay. That sounds pretty bad. But even if that did happen (it still might not), you could still pick up and carry on, right?"

This is not an invitation to dismiss or minimize your feelings. Rather, when you turn and face your biggest fear head on and remind yourself that it really wouldn't be the utter collapse of the known universe, it doesn't seem so unmanageable after all. When we are awash in anxiety, we give outcomes power over us; we say that there is a potential outcome that is totally unbearable and unmanageable. But is this true? Is there *really* an outcome that is unmanageable?

Keep asking, "What's so bad about that?"

> "They'll all gossip about me."
>
> "What's so bad about that?"
>
> "I'll be shunned. They won't invite me out anymore."
>
> "And what's so bad about that?"
>
> "They'll think I'm a bad person!"
>
> "What's so bad about that?"
>
> "Well, nothing, I guess. I suppose it won't kill me to have some people not like me . . ."

Anxiety can often be nipped in the bud when you realize that a bad outcome isn't unbearable. So many imagined problems and fears actually can't hurt you at all, and you don't have to spend your life trying to avoid that discomfort!

> "But this is serious. I could lose both my arms and legs and never be able to walk again."
>
> "Okay. So that's the worst that could happen? That's pretty bad. But even then you'd be able to choose your reaction. Even then you'd have some options, and some things to be happy about. So, even the worst possible outcome can be dealt with, if necessary."

The truth is, the worst case very seldom happens, anyway. Realizing that you always have power and options, no matter the outcome, takes away the sting of catastrophic thinking. Sometimes, people who have actually endured a catastrophe express this sentiment—they've proven to themselves that they *can* recover from even the worst life has to offer. What's more empowering and confidence-boosting than that?

Takeaways

- Once we are firmly in our accepting, aware "observing self," we can begin to rethink our cognitive distortions, expectations, inner myths and narratives, assumptions, and biases. We don't *challenge* them, exactly, but make space for alternatives that we choose consciously.
- We can practice cognitive restructuring by first becoming aware of the way we think and shining consciousness onto what has been previously automatic, habitual, and unconscious. When we can shift our perspective and gently change our self-concept, we start to think, feel, and behave differently, and this change is not superficial or mere "positive thinking."
- After awareness, we can adjust, dispute, or engage with our thoughts and consciously choose alternatives. We can then play these alternatives out in our real lives. We do not need to judge ourselves, fix anything, or find out the "truth," but instead appraise our thoughts according to how useful they are in achieving our goals, set in accordance to our deepest values.

- The two-column technique can help us slow down, identify automatic negative thoughts, and restructure them consciously. This takes patience, courage, compassion, and curiosity. Look for all-or-nothing thinking, catastrophizing, mind-reading, trying to predict the future, making generalizations, or extreme negative appraisals. Reword these thoughts or even consider how they may be converted into useful action.
- There are countless techniques for cognitive restructuring, but they all begin with awareness and end with our willingness to genuinely entertain alternatives. We can use Socratic questioning (keep asking after evidence for assumptions and beliefs, keep asking why), guided imagery (to rehearse or flesh out alternatives, past or future), record-keeping or journaling (to put thoughts down and play around with alternatives), and experimenting with "what-if?" (to follow catastrophizing to its logical conclusion and see if discomfort, failure, or uncertainty are really all that bad).
- Cognitive restructuring can help us cultivate a perspective and mindset that is proactive and less anxiety-filled by design.

CHAPTER 4

All We Have Is Now

Have you ever noticed how some people rush through life in a constant near-panic, trying to organize and sort out and control every little thing, almost as though they had appointed themselves the CEO of the very universe, which would crumble to a chaotic mess if they weren't there to take charge? Maybe you are that person?

Panic, worry, overthinking, and rumination are certainly a sign of a mind overrun with cognitive distortions or a perspective that blows the negative out of proportion. And anxiety is definitely a question of narrowed focus and lack of awareness. But in this chapter, we'll consider that anxiety can also go deeper than this and speak to a more basic orientation to life itself; i.e., one where we fundamentally lack *trust* in our world.

Whether you call it trust, acceptance, tolerance, grace, or surrender, there is an attitude characterized by a deference to those things that are in fact outside your control or understanding. Let's say you practice becoming more aware and gain mastery over those cognitive distortions that are holding you back. Let's say you're completely comfortable in the present, fully alert and conscious, and in a perfectly proactive and open frame of mind. And then some idiot walks by and insults you.

The fact is, life is positively brimming with situations that we cannot change, no matter how much we dislike or disagree with them. Loss is inevitable. We don't always get our way. Sometimes, things are unfair and there is no justice, no matter how much you rail against it. Sometimes, life is confusing and difficult and no answers seem forthcoming, no matter how deeply into it all you look. What then?

A crucial part of a calm, equanimous life is to learn to accept. When we fight and rage against a reality we wish didn't exist, or when we play "CEO of the world" and assume that everything is our responsibility, we are anxious. When parts of the world, as they are, are deemed unacceptable to you, then you position yourself in fear and resistance. Only when we accept can we have any peace or freedom.

Think about it this way: What is happening is already happening. The way things are is the way they are. You are already not in control. If you flap and fuss and stress about this fact, you may create the *illusion* that you are in control of it all, but what is happening will continue to happen, only you will also be unhappy and anxious. So, you are in this way choosing to be unhappy and creating your own unhappiness.

Now, this can all sound very Zen and detached—surely you have *some* control over life? Absolutely. But where you don't? There is literally no other choice, so why not accept, embrace, flow with it, and surrender? It is usually just the ego which wants to barge in and say, "No! That's not how things should be!" and try to dictate terms to reality itself. But does acting like the whole world is your enemy bring you an ounce more happiness? If you can relax and let go of the need to argue, justify, complain, explain, control, fix, and predict . . . then you simultaneously drop the ego, and who knows, maybe you even find something new and joyful you didn't expect.

On a deeper level, as human beings, we tend to look at things we don't understand or the things we can't control as threats. We see them as things that take away our power, hurt us, or insult the vision we have of ourselves as all-powerful. But is it really true that you always know best? Is it really true that the thing you want in any moment is really reasonable, justifiable, or wise? Is it really possible for you, as you are now, to comprehend all the bigger pictures that you are a part of and confidently say what should and shouldn't be the case?

Humility is actually a supremely comfortable attitude to hold. It's the relaxation we feel when we stop resisting against things that are not our business to resist. If left to its own devices, your mind will conjure its stories—any stories—and find things to push against, to be afraid of, to desire, and to wonder about. When we are anxious, it's like we are a problem looking for a place to happen!

Surrender Is Easy

First of all, acceptance isn't hard. It isn't a punishing, near-impossible superhuman feat. Rather, it's what you choose *not* to do. Say you're in a movie theater and a rude kid starts screaming. You get irritated, automatically, unconsciously. There and then, you have a fight with reality. Where does your resistance come from? No, it's not a natural fact. It's not coming from the rude kid, but from your mind. So why does your mind do that?

Well, deep down lies the unconscious belief that our resistance is a kind of problem-solving tool, or that if we are unhappy, this will in one way or another resolve the issue. That if we fight and push back, then maybe we can have peace, or things will go our way. This assumption is false, however—does it really make sense to resolve unhappiness by getting unhappy about it? Nope.

It's not that you shrug and smugly say, "Well, everything is the way it should be." There is no should. There is just *is*.

What would your inner world feel like if you genuinely believed that everything is just right, as it is, and doesn't need you to decide whether it should be that way or not? What if you stopped thinking it was your business to decide how reality should play out? For many of us, the fear is that we will be obliterated, or that everything will fall to pieces. Instead, what happens is that we simply . . . live. Things happen, and we flow with them. Without resistance.

"So, if I'm being eaten alive by mosquitos, am I just supposed to sit there and let them do it?"

You could. You could also get up and move away from them, or fetch bug repellent. But notice how no solution truly requires you to fiercely beat your chest and yell at the world, "This isn't right! I'm not supposed to be bitten by a mosquito, ever!" If you have already been bitten by a mosquito, arguing that you shouldn't have been is even more useless.

We will experience pain and discomfort. But we can choose to let that flow through and out of us. As they say, what you resist, persists. Imagine again the stranger that insulted you out of nowhere. A brief moment of discomfort, then it passes. But if you are full of resistance to this event, you end up fuming and stewing over it days later—long after the stranger and his insult have passed. So, resistance actually creates more of what we don't want, whereas acceptance makes room for what is . . . and lets it go so it can flow on.

Suffering and resistance don't serve any purpose.

What Does Acceptance Actually Look Like?

All we have is now. And that's all we have to accept. What is, now. You don't have to accept what might happen tomorrow, or what has already been and gone, or the hypothetical stories your brain is making up for you. You are simply in the moment, not desperately trying to run away from it or add to it. Let's say you're in a bad situation. You're unhappy, you're in pain, you're scared. Okay. Be that way. After all, if you are resistant to those feelings, you are giving yourself twice as much to carry—the initial discomfort plus the discomfort of not being allowed to feel discomfort.

Remember that it's an illusion that suffering solves problems or changes anything for us. More often, plainly and openly acknowledging the situation we are in is precisely what allows us to move on from it with creative and reasonable solutions. It's only a story we tell ourselves that we should be happy all the time, or that being confused or tired is a problem we need to solve urgently. When you realize this, you often see that the confusion or tiredness or pain is not so bad on its own—it's the resistance that hurts most! Can you look at your present moment and just say yes to it, without needing to bring your mind for appraisal and judgment and interpretation?

Doing this is the same as creating "space", as discussed in an earlier chapter. Instead of forcing the present moment to conform to our ego's wishes, we simply become curious about what is unfolding. Practicing acceptance doesn't mean we are immobile or fail to take action. We do act! But we don't act from a sense of anxious desperation. We don't act to avoid or resist or deny. When we stop anxiously clinging to always needing to *do something*, we can actually start to see things more clearly. Can we change the situation? If so, we do it. If not, we accept. Nothing is wrong, nothing is a mistake.

So, how can we concretely practice all this in everyday life? Well, you have the opportunity to do it right now—in this moment. Pause right now and take a look at the present moment, and see if you can *accept* it as it is. Notice everything that's there . . . maybe shoulder tension, maybe a lingering bad mood, maybe anticipation for something coming later today, maybe a nagging memory of something you need to do at 4 o'clock, or maybe your perception of the dogs barking next door.

Now, just unhook your story-telling brain from all of this for a second and merely be present. You might say something out loud like, "I don't mind," or "Okay," just to drive home the feeling of you relinquishing the need to control or steer or interpret or judge. If intrusive thoughts pop up, say "Okay" again. Even your resistance is part of the moment. Accept that, too. Just feel the full, perfect-as-it-is moment that needs nothing.

You can practice this anytime you like. When you feel anxiety spiraling out of control or a bad mood descending, try this exercise. Remind yourself that your only job for the moment is just to *allow* everything to be what it is! Simple, right?

- When you don't know something, simply and plainly say, "I don't know." It's okay not to understand or control everything.
- Notice the desire for perfection and gently let it go. Try to find three wonderful things about

the present moment as it is, without needing intervention or improvement.

- Be aware of a tendency to want to force conclusions or hurry along to resolve uncertainties. It might take some effort to remind yourself often: "None of us knows what will happen tomorrow."
- You can practice giving up anxious control in small ways—ask others for help and then try to trust that they know what they're doing. Delegate tasks to others. Allow yourself to be taken care of. Ask for someone's opinion and genuinely entertain the idea that they could be right.
- Be patient. If you notice yourself getting hurried and rushed, stop, take a deep breath and ask whether the situation is really an emergency, or whether it's just your ego's desire for control and certainty. Where did your timeline come from, anyway?
- Bring more flexibility into your life. Instead of being angry that a situation isn't what you want, try to move around it, explore it, and look at it from different perspectives. Is there another equally workable alternative, or a solution you haven't considered yet? If you're too busy having a tantrum about not getting your way, you might miss the opportunity to get something better!
- If you make a mistake, say, "I made a mistake," and then let it go. You can learn from it, certainly. But forgiving yourself is about choosing not to carry

the weight of that mistake with yourself forever.

- At the very least, laugh at yourself. When you're hung up on feeling proud and filled with ego, it's easier to feel humiliated or shamed. Just let that all go. Is it really the end of the world if you embarrass yourself now and then? In fact, isn't it a bit funny, when you really think about it?
- Remember that suffering doesn't actually solve any problems. It certainly doesn't make you a good person and won't get you what you want. So, notice when you are blaming others, complaining without taking action to help yourself, or playing the martyr in an unconscious attempt to have others come and save you. If you feel bad, take a good look at that feeling and ask, "What does it actually achieve?" Do you really want to feel bad, *recreationally*?
- Many people find calmness and serenity in surrendering to their concept of God or embracing the spiritual side of life to counteract anxiety. It can feel supremely relaxing and grounding to know that you are part of something bigger and infinitely more complex than you can ever comprehend. Whatever that looks like for you, spare a moment every day to ask if there is some higher power or force out there that you are happy to relinquish control to . . . at least temporarily.
- Stop *judging* yourself and others. This is the most common way we interject our own assumptions

and try to control reality. Just tell yourself that it is not your responsibility to sit in judgment of things, or decide what is good and what isn't. It's just not your job. Trust that the world can unfold as it does without you sitting and allocating value judgments to things. If you find yourself feeling angry and impatient with the flaws of others, quickly remind yourself of your own shortcomings—and then understand that both you and others deserve compassion and understanding.

- Remember to stay grateful. With the attitude of gratitude, you remember that your life was given to you for free, and that it is constantly sustained by countless miracles you cannot comprehend in the least, all given in abundance. Turn your attention to all the ways that life is wonderful just as it is and cultivate contentment and appreciation, rather than always grumbling and looking for the next thing you feel is wrong, or which you're entitled to. All we have is now—but that's a *lot*!
- Finally, take frequent breaks. Life can be hard, but we don't always have to go at it white-knuckled and forceful. Make sure you build in enough time in life to contemplate, to relax, to go soft within, and to simply be receptive rather than in active problem-solving mode.

Making a Home in the Here and Now

I want to introduce you to two "places":

The first place is called Elsewhere, with sprawling neighborhoods all over the place, primarily in the past and in the future. This is a place you visit by identfying with your constantly churning "monkey mind." It's made up of words—memories, dreams, fears, hypotheticals, beliefs, thoughts, conditionals, guesses, narratives, interpretations, judgments, personal myths, symbols, concerns, hopes, and so on. The most important thing about this first place is that *it doesn't exist.* Not really. In a very real sense, this place is dead.

The second place is called Here and Now, and it has just one small (but deceptively spacious) room, based eternally in the present moment. You visit this place using your body, the five senses in your body, and most of all by using your sense of calm, focused awareness on what is. The most important thing about this second place is that it is always changing, flowing, unfolding, and becoming. It is always brand spanking new and yet it's old as time and has always been here. Joy, meaning, purpose, and connection all happen in this second place. In a very real sense, this place is alive. It *is* life.

When you live in Elsewhere, yours is an existence of anxiety, resistance, and friction. The brain is a powerful organ, and it can conjure up anything it likes. It usually conjures up complicated visions that we get snared in and distracted by. It conjures up a self-concept, and tells stories about what is allowed and what isn't. It puts meanings on events. It spins stories about things to be afraid of in the future. It tells stories about what has already happened, and keeps on telling them so we don't forget.

When people are anxious, they mistakenly think that what's bothering them is LIFE. They think the conditions of life are difficult and challenging, and they push against it. But the truth is, their problem is not with life, because, frankly, that's not where they are. Their difficulty comes from engaging not with life, but with the pictures and words their minds conjure for them; i.e., they are struggling with living in that other place, Elsewhere. They wrestle with problems of their own creation, and assume that it's life itself that is the problem. But life is sitting there, minding its own business in the present moment, being completely ignored!

When you are battling anxiety, you are usually wrestling with demons that live Elsewhere. When you are still and simply living in the Here and Now, you deal with life as it really is.

A simple example will illustrate this: I had a friend who had a very funny habit. Let's say we went out together for a nice long walk in the sunny woods, and it was amazingly beautiful. They'd say, "Oh, gosh, this is nice, we should really do walks more often, shouldn't we? Or we should do a proper hike and camping as well. But when? One day, let's do a really long camp in the mountains or something. It'll be winter soon and then we won't have sun, so we'd better make a plan soon . . ."

I say this was a funny habit because all the while they spoke, my friend was missing the fact that *we were already having a good time!* They were so caught up in ideas of what could and should and might happen in the future that the present moment, the beautiful, perfect present moment, was whizzing right by them, and they were oblivious to it.

This shows you how powerful the mind is—powerful enough to carry you cleanly away from the moment, even if that moment is precisely the thing your brain thought it was helping you create. I bet my friend created for themselves a real sense of "life passing them by" or a feeling that time was running out. But it never was. They were just living Elsewhere.

In the case of my friend, this habit is relatively harmless. But it isn't always. How many of us live *permanently* in this Elsewhere zone? We say things like, "I can't do that; I'm not that kind of person," because we are clinging tightly to a memory of what we're like instead of encountering the fact of who we are right now, in the present. We become the person who slaves away at a job they hate, throwing all their present moments away, because they cannot stop thinking about some mythical, non-existent place called the future where they'd better have a good retirement.

Isn't it funny how human beings go out of their way to torment themselves with memories of the past or worries of the future? You would think it strange if a person deliberately sat down every evening to watch a terrifying horror movie that disturbed them, over and over again. Yet, aren't we doing that when we idly catastrophize about the future? You could sit there, in your living room, on a comfy sofa . . . and yet be absolutely immobilized with terror. People know that moving pictures and words on a screen are not real, and yet don't we take the moving pictures and words in our heads as though they were reality itself?

Let's approach this idea from another angle. Picture a really delicious meal from a fancy five-star restaurant. You could sit there and eat it without really tasting it, and instead feast on the memory of a disgusting meal you once had when you were six years old. You could sit there with a mouth full of delicious food and think, "Nothing good ever happens to me," or "What's that waiter's problem, anyway?" or "People who waste money on fancy food like this are being stupid."

Or . . . you could enjoy the meal. Each bite of it. Here and now. Because that's the only place that meal exists—in the here and now.

Everywhere else? That's the zone of worry and rumination and denial and endless churning thoughts. The zone of problems.

Try this right now. In this very moment—yes, this one right now!—genuinely ask yourself if anything is wrong with your life. What is missing, really? It might feel like there's a mountain of problems, but ask honestly how many of these are just *thoughts about life,* and not life itself. When you trim those away and look just at the present, it's pretty, isn't it? Your brain imagines things, and those things feel like they're real and present . . . but are they? What is *really present* right now? Just you and the moment.

Let's get comfortable in the here and now. Let's see what life looks like when we live here, and not Elsewhere.

Pain Versus Suffering

Well, maybe in your immediate present you find you have a bad flu and feel like hell. Okay. Your head hurts, you're uncomfortable and your throat burns. This is pain.

If you sulk and rage and pout about the fact that you are sick, start churning thoughts, start resisting the present, start arguing reality, or start getting carried away with how you shouldn't be sick—that is suffering.

Pain is a natural, unavoidable part of life. It happens in the present. It's fleeting. Suffering is avoidable and is of our own making. It happens everywhere but the present. It can remain even after the pain flows away and dissipates.

Suffering is non-acceptance of the moment, or clinging to or escaping from the truth. Suffering is a story about pain.

If you have the flu, you're in pain. If you say, "I deserve this for being stupid and staying out in the rain and catching a bug," then you have the pain and another extra thing called suffering. Your poor brain is trying to help with all this explaining and judging and controlling. It wants to predict the future and learn and operate with a stable sense of self. It wants to be in charge! But this can sometimes mean it creates suffering for itself.

If you are avoiding the present, skimming over it, fighting with it, or in a daydream about what happened yesterday or what could happen tomorrow, you miss out on the full, rich beauty of the present moment. You miss all the perfection and contentment right under your nose because you're anxiously solving the problem of how to have more contentment in your life. You become the person that treats the present moment like a waiting room and a place to linger while the better thing—the future—comes along eventually. You say, "As soon as XYZ happens, then I'll be happy." The present is always inadequate and always a stepping-stone to something better, *Elsewhere.* You are not enough, the present moment is not enough, and the entirety of life itself is just a means to an end. Can you see how crazy it is to throw away all of life in favor of the future/past—which, after all, is just a thought: just a little flutter in your brain?

> "When I retire, then I'll live the life I always wanted."
>
> "I should have studied further; my life would be so different now."
>
> "I'll get around to it . . . just as soon as we've moved house."

Your life is not a dress rehearsal. It's really happening. And it's really happening *right now.*

Your Anchor to the Present: The Body

How does one live in the now?

Remember that Elsewhere is accessed via the mind—we travel to the past, the future, or a hypothetical and imagined present using our thoughts and ideas.

The Here and Now, though, is only accessed one way: through the body.

It's really a wonderful insight to realize that your body is always and only ever in the present moment, so if you tune into it, you will be right there in the now with it. Your five senses can be thought of anchors that ground you into the real now and the environment all around you. In your senses, you realize how much richness and depth is in the eternal moment—so much to see, smell, hear, and touch without ever needing to escape into the abstract and non-real world of the mind.

This dimension is real and alive in a way that mental activity can never be. When we are here, we are living. When we are in our heads, we're thinking about living and playing with images and ideas of life—it's like trying to eat the word "cake" instead of actually, literally tasting that delicious frosting on our tongues.

How do you live in the now? Simply ask your anxious mind to get out of the way and allow your body to do what it already knows how to do.

Can you look and see without labeling?

Move Your Body, Still Your Mind

Many prominent trauma therapists and theorists now believe that trauma is really anxiety *trapped* in the body. When we are afraid, confronted with danger, or threatened, the natural and healthy response is to take action—fight back, run away, or make a plan to reduce the impact of the trouble. If we are prevented from getting into our bodies and literally moving, the anxiety remains in our body. No longer able to power beneficial action, that anxious energy is turned inward and wreaks havoc on us. We stay stuck in the past, replaying old memories, never able to fully release tension and move on. A great way to release trauma and stress from the body is to physically, literally *move* it out of you. Don't sit down and talk about abstract ideas and thoughts *about* the anxiety—after all, that is just more thought traffic, more anxiety, and more rumination. Instead, get into your body and move. There are two ways to engage the body in the management of anxiety:

The first is a **short-term** approach: If you are stressed, shocked, alarmed or worried, become conscious of this fact and deliberately try to move to release the tension. Get out and go for a long, hard run. Put on your favorite dance music and move energetically and vigorously in your living room. Get on your hands and knees and scrub the bathroom. Do some yoga to stretch out those muscles and release any tension you've been holding in your neck or hips. If you like, close the door and punch a pillow! You could combine this with some visualization and actively imagine that stress and worry is leaving your body as you move.

Think of anxiety and mental tension as pent-up energy—energy that is valuable and useful if channeled into action. Sometimes, after moving this way, you'll feel as though things "shift" internally and you suddenly have an insight, feel motivated to take action, or have an idea for a way to solve a problem.

The second is a **long-term** approach: If anxiety and overthinking are a chronic problem for you, you might like to make sure that you're regularly checking in with the rest of your being, below your neck! Worrywarts and overthinkers tend to live in their heads. The antidote is to reconnect to the body. Your body is intelligent—it can find its own equilibrium without the intervention of your conscious, rational mind!

For chronic worry, make sure that you're regularly engaging your body in as many ways as possible. Instead of thinking about life, *do it.* Get a monthly massage (this will help you cultivate that all-important sense of surrender, too!). Take up regular dance practice, do tai chi or yoga, or enhance your body-mind connection by doing martial arts, sports, or simple aerobics. Climb a tree like you did when you were a kid. If it gets your body moving and makes you smile, then schedule it in.

A Sensory Meditation

Think of your being as a radio that can only be tuned into one station at a time—either the thinking and ruminating mind, or the anchored and present consciousness, aware of the flow of life coming in through the senses. It's one or the other. When you do the following sensory meditation, you are calming the overthinking mind and strengthening the part of you that lives in the delicious, ever-unfolding present. Here's how to do it.

Once a day (or as often as you can), give yourself the task of completely, utterly immersing yourself in a sensory experience. It doesn't matter what it is. It could be that you spend a full five minutes relishing the many subtle flavors and textures when eating a ripe, juicy pear. It could be that you close your eyes and focus every atom of your awareness on a beautiful, touching piece of music. It could be that you sit quietly and simply breathe, savoring the sensations of the breath entering and leaving your lungs.

Find something that pleases or interests you and sit with it, with no intention other than to be fully, completely present with it, in your senses. Take your time. Really notice what you are doing. Imagine you are doing this ordinary, everyday thing for the first time, or that you are a newborn baby and have never even used your senses before.

In time, this practice will convince you how endless and infinite the present moment is. How deep and enthralling it is to simply stay inside it and feel all its contours. When we are rushed and anxious and identify with the mind, the present moment seems paltry and uninteresting. Practicing sensory awareness like this reminds us of the unbelievable riches that are all around us, if we only we pause long enough to truly sense them.

This will automatically create calmness and serenity in you, and quiet the busy and stressed-out mind.

Takeaways

- Panic, worry, rumination, anxiety, and overthinking can stem from over-identifying with the inner mental chatter and narratives we have about life, which are often filled with cognitive distortions, biases, illusory expectations, fears, and sheer irrationality. Our brain can conjure up stressful mental activity in the past or the future, but calmness and serenity only occur in one place: the present.
- All we have is now. Surrender, acceptance, and calm awareness in the present doesn't mean we are passive or giving up—if we can act, we act. If we can't, we accept it. There is no need for anxiety or rumination. Remember that anxiety and overthinking don't actually solve problems for us or help us in any way, even if our brain convinces us that we need to rush in and control everything.
- Getting comfortable with the present moment means practicing patience, humility, humor, tolerance of the uncertain, and flexibility to respond to the moment rather than react to or resist it.
- Pain is inevitable and fleeting. But suffering is in our response to pain, and is avoidable. If we cling to pain by resisting it, telling stories about it, or

repeatedly pulling it back into the moment from the past, we are creating suffering for ourselves. Calm, proactive people accept pain and let it pass and don't allow themselves to get caught up in unnecessary suffering.

- Your physical body, your five senses, and your conscious awareness are anchors in the present moment. You can be in the Here and Now rather than Elsewhere whenever you anchor into the present moment via the body. Still a busy mind by moving your body (such as with physical activity), or do sensory meditation to slow down and connect to the present again.

CHAPTER 5

There Is No Black and White

In this chapter, we're going to shift focus a little and consider an aspect of overthinking that might be depressingly familiar to some. We've spoken at length about turning up to the present moment with quiet awareness and without judgment, labelling, or interpretation. Anxiety can certainly take the form of worry for the future or regret for the past, but for some of us, our rumination and overthinking comes down to a very particular kind of cognitive distortion: judgment.

Judgment for the self or others? Well, they may be one and the same!

Judgment is simple: It's any time we look at what **is** and what we think **should be,** and make a comparison. You'll recognize this as plain old avoidance, non-acceptance, or arguing with reality. We can direct this toward ourselves ("I'm struggling. I'm not supposed to be struggling. This is a problem. It means I'm a bad person"), or we can direct it toward others ("They were mean to me, and it isn't supposed to be that way. It's a problem. They're a problem").

When we judge, it impacts our ability to accept, love, and have compassion for ourselves and others. It narrows our focus, makes us anxious, and makes us focus on the negative. When we allow our ego to jump in with a big story about what should be, then we sometimes confuse actions and events with reality itself—for example, if someone was mean to us once, we conclude that they are fundamentally mean as a person, forever. We stop relating to them as they are in the moment, full of potential, and start relating to the *story* we have of them, or a memory, or a role we assign them. We forget we've done this and then fail to update our stories!

But as we've seen, pure attention and awareness without judgment is the key to being calm and content. It also makes you nicer to be around and far more accepting of yourself!

How To Be Less Judgmental

Dropping judgment is not something we do just to be nice to others. We do it for us and for our own health and peace of mind. If we judge others, chances are we turn the same attitude onto ourselves, creating unhappiness, stress, and discontent.

When we meditate and try to encounter the moment as it is, what we are doing is turning to every new sensation and saying, "Hello! Who are you? You're interesting. Welcome. I accept you." We don't try to label or categorize the sensation or decide whether it's good or bad, whether we like it or not, what it means, where it's leading, whether it "should" be happening or not, and so on.

When we drop judgment, we also give ourselves the chance to be this way to *ourselves and others.* When we encounter another human being, we can do the equivalent: "Hello! Who are you? You're interesting. Welcome. I accept you," regardless of whether we've known them twenty years or just met them. Regardless of whether they agree with us or not, what they're wearing or doing or saying, and whatever their opinion is of us. We face them as they are in the moment and suspend our ego's desire to come to a pronouncement.

We might face ourselves in the here and now and say the same thing. "Hello! Who are you today?" You forget about what happened yesterday. You don't label yourself. You don't assume that because you failed yesterday you will fail today. You don't hold on to stories and expectations about what you can and cannot do. You have no history, no role. You just encounter yourself as you are, alive, in the moment.

When we encounter ourselves or others, we can often skip right over their genuine nature in the moment in favor of a bunch of nonsense in our heads:

> We might confuse their temporary behavior with who they are in an absolute sense. ("That guy who yelled at me in traffic is probably a jerk 24/7.")

We might think assume that they are whatever their categories and labels and types say they are. ("Oh, he's Swedish. He's probably really organized and efficient.")

We might have an emotional reaction to them and forever more interpret them through that lens. ("My father bullied me all throughout my childhood. I don't care what he has to say now; he's dead to me.")

We might continually and unconsciously force them into a fixed narrative about their identity as we see it. ("My little sister is the baby of the family! I know she's thirty-nine now and a mother, but when I see her, I can't help calling her by her embarrassing childhood nickname.")

We might think that difference or strangeness is wrong or threatening. ("She follows that weird religion. She's nuts, and I wouldn't trust her.")

But instead of all this shorthand and assumption-making, we can actually do something else: perceive what is right in front of us. Judgment comes from our mind, whereas when we are in pure consciousness, in the moment, we don't judge—we just experience. We notice that people are complex, dynamic, and usually quite lovable! If you constantly look at others or yourself and only see what you think *should* be there, you are blind to what *is* there. How could you make real connections, and how could you have a peaceful relationship with yourself with this perspective?

So many of us are having constant arguments with pictures and thoughts of people, and not with people themselves. We walk around with a vision of who we wish we were or think we should be or hope we could be, all the while missing the wonderful thing we actually are. It is as though our masks are talking to their masks, and the people underneath the masks never truly see or know one another.

Conflict and trouble come along with the stories we make. Our interpretations and value judgments are automatic, and they help us make sense of the world, ourselves, and other people. But they also shut us out from all those things! Because people are not the thoughts we have about them. They are real, living, changing, and amazingly complex beings. Like you!

Here's a great practice for being less judgmental with other people (and ultimately with yourself): *Stick to the facts.* Not interpretations, value judgments, categorizations, or reactions. Just facts. Just things in their "is-ness." Just people as they are in the here and now.

Let's look at an example. You are walking behind someone in the street and see them toss a chocolate wrapper onto the ground and walk off. You immediately get angry and indignant and go into judgment mode. "What a pig! He has no respect. I hate people who litter; it's just so rude." Well, you've told a nice little story with a villain and a hero (you), and you're fully engrossed in the feeling of rage and injustice. You go further, though. "People these days have no manners at all. The world is going to seed. I despair. It's a lack of education or something. Honestly, this is why the planet is in the mess it is—nobody cares! Nobody takes care of things."

Wow! What a story. Let's look closely. What has actually happened? *Just the facts?*

Someone dropped a chocolate wrapper on the street. That's it. The rest? All judgment. All an argument with reality. All our ego marching in to say how things should be. Incidentally, it's a whole lot of anxiety, too!

You could stop in this moment and consider that you are, again, not the CEO of the universe. You can reject the present moment and how it is, along with the person in the moment with you, or you can accept who and what they are. There's a chocolate wrapper on the street. You choose to bring your mind in to label it as evil, lazy, selfish. These labels make you anxious and unhappy—not the wrapper on the street.

In this brief moment, you have gone to war with a fellow human being. You have summoned up feelings of hate and injustice against them. You are no longer in the moment; you are completely in the story you've spun, and it's an ugly story. The mind, trying to be helpful, thinks that it's necessary to judge and compartmentalize everything. But think about it: Is it really a matter of urgent importance that you sit and decide who the goodies and baddies are in life? Does it really help you in any way to decide that *you* are the goodie or the baddie? We assume that our judgment somehow makes the world go around. We think that being judgmental means having taste or opinions, or even a personality.

Perhaps we think that our entire self will disintegrate if we don't know who we are better than or who we disagree with!

The trouble is, all of this comes at a price: It makes us anxious and unhappy.

The next time you are with someone else, try to focus on *just the facts*. Listen to the words the person is saying. Look at their face. Feel what's it like to be in the moment with them. Imagine you have never met them before and this is the first time you are knowing them. Really, if you are fully in the moment, you *are* meeting them as strangers anew, every single second!

When judgment comes up, just look at it and see it there. See it getting in the way of your perception of the moment.

> "He's an old guy. Everyone from his generation is like that. How boring!"
>
> "Dumb blonde."
>
> "He's got rich parents; he's never had to work hard like I have."
>
> "She's actually a huge racist, and I have no time for people like that."
>
> "Did you see the gift they brought? Oh my God. Shocking."

Just notice it. Notice how the story of a person is actually different from the person themselves, living and breathing in the moment. See if you can consciously choose to set the story aside for a moment and simply be with the person again, in the moment. Today's world is full of divisions and invitations to engage in "us versus them" thinking. These are just doorways to more anxiety and unhappiness.

Now, there's nothing to say you can't have genuine, present-based emotions around an interaction. If someone is currently being a jerk to you, well, notice that. But watch for the tendency to add additional layers of your own on top:

Don't assume. When you fill in missing information, you inject your own bias into the picture. Just look at the picture. They laughed. That's a fact. But it is your assumption that they laughed because they were making fun of you.

Don't interpret. You don't really know why things happen. They didn't message you. That's all. Believing that this "means" X, Y, or Z is an interpretation that comes from your head, not the situation in front of you.

Don't be on the defensive. Instead, assume everyone is doing the best they can and don't make an enemy of the world, other people, or yourself. When you're on the defensive, you see threats everywhere.

Don't expect. If you are anticipating what will happen, making predictions, or waiting for a particular outcome, you are not present. You are simply hurrying the moment along to a foregone conclusion. You are not a director of the play of life! Let it unfold. Let it surprise you.

Don't mind-read. When we guess at what's in someone's head, we reduce the dynamism and complexity of the moment to a simplified, incorrect story.

One way to reduce the tendency to do all of the above is to become **curious**: Ask questions about the person or situation in front of you. Instead of barging ahead as though you already know everything about the person and the situation, be humble and assume you actually know nothing. Allow people to change. Let them expand and contain contradictions. Let them be different from you. Let them be confusing or unintelligible. Who says you need to understand people, anyway? You can still have compassion and love for them all the same!

Having expectations is a recipe for disappointment. And having expectations of other people is a recipe for judgment. If you find yourself going into judgment of someone, stop, take a breath, and push yourself to appreciate something else about them. Fine, they just said something annoying which you had a reaction to. But can you just make room for them and for yourself being annoyed, and turn your attention to all the things that you can acknowledge and appreciate in them right now?

When the Person You Judge Is Yourself

The way we encounter others is exactly the way we encounter ourselves. That harsh and judgmental voice you project onto others? It's the same voice you have in your own head when you encounter yourself. Being self-critical and having low self-esteem often comes down to the same non-acceptance and resistance to reality we've been discussing throughout this book.

We look at the reality of who we are, and cannot accept who we are, as we are. Instead, we get carried away with expectations, assumptions, interpretations, and endless stories. We compare ourselves to a million "shoulds" and find ourselves wanting. It's no secret that this creates nothing but anxiety and dissatisfaction.

Often, the self-help world's answer to self-judgment is to go in the opposite direction: "self-love." But actually, you don't need to love yourself. What a relief! After all, praising who you are and feeling that you're awesome is also making a judgment. You are comparing what is and what should be and finding that they match nicely, and so this means you are allowed to feel good about yourself.

This could work—temporarily. But a far more lasting and deeply satisfying approach is to drop all "shoulds" entirely and really and truly embrace what is. Can you have the courage to feel okay in yourself, calm, contented, and still *with you being exactly as you are*? This is deeper than confidence or self-love. If, one day, you find yourself in a rotten mood, and you feel bad about who you are, could you embrace *that feeling*? So many of us think self-love and compassion sounds like a good idea—but we reserve it for later (Elsewhere . . .). If we discover in the moment that we in fact hate ourselves and feel bad, we think there's a problem, that something is wrong, and we resist it all.

But what happens when we embrace and accept the moment—**whatever it is**?

If we are feeling angry and upset? We accept that.

If we are feeling happy and hopeful? We accept that.

If we are feeling undecided and confused? We accept that.

If we are feeling like we cannot possibly accept how we are currently feeling? We accept that, too.

Whatever arises in the moment, there we are with calm, alert compassion and curious attention. That's it. Notice your mind jumping in to say, "Sure, *one day* I'll be a wonderful calm person who accepts themselves . . ." Notice your mind springing into action: "Wait! It can't be that simple. There has to be some sort of problem here . . ." Look at yourself doing all this and accept even that.

The Judgment Off-Switch: Non-Duality

The Buddhists have something to teach us about the deepest roots of judgment and all the anxiety and suffering it creates for us. Discussions of non-duality can get abstract and philosophical very quickly, but the concepts themselves are simple.

There is Yin, and there is Yang. There is no problem.

We live in a world of duality—there is good and bad, up and down, life and death, black and white. These opposites imply one another and rely on one another—

there is no happy without sad. Nothing stands alone, but in constant, changing relation to its opposite. We know it's day because it's not night. So, day and night are in a fundamental, irreducible relationship with one another. There is no problem.

What does this mean for anxiety and rumination? And what does it tell us about our tendency to judge ourselves and others?

At the core of every judgment is duality:

> "They're wrong." (And I'm right.)
>
> "This is such an unfortunate accident." (That is, it's not deliberate or desirable.)
>
> "That is a perfect outfit." (Others are not so perfect.)

The mind is like a knife that slices the wholeness of reality into two parts: this and that. We see a person do something, we call that something "bad," and then we cut that person and their actions off from the whole. They now belong to the bad group, which is separate from the good group. We do it to ourselves, too. We look at something within (a feeling, a thought) and decide, for example, that it's unacceptable. Our mind cuts it off, and we set it apart from the rest of us. The mind, in its judgment, creates these cuts and divisions, but they are an illusion—the thing was always *whole.*

When we forget that everything is whole, then we can shut down our compassion, narrow our awareness, and start to find enemies and things to push against. We stop seeing that we are all part of humanity, and start to see races, sexes, political groups, and nations. We stop seeing ourselves as full, complex wholes, and start seeing ourselves as a collection of good parts and bad parts, strengths and weaknesses, things to be proud of and things to be ashamed of. And all of this slicing and dicing is very, very stressful!

When we are living with duality, everything is split, and when we have two halves, we automatically judge which half is better. And from that comes anxiety, disappointment, entitlement, and the whole saga of *should* and *have to* and so on. We are again in the overthinking monkey mind, we are outside of the present moment, and we are living in stories and ruminations. And what good is a story if it doesn't have a problem and a solution, a bad guy and a good guy, Team A and Team B?

> *On the one hand, we have:*
>
> Duality, judgment, stories, non-acceptance of the present, division, and anxiety.
>
> *On the other, we have:*
>
> Non-duality, acceptance, being present with what is, wholeness, ease, and contentment.

To put this into conscious practice, we have to realize that judgement comes from duality, and duality is based in language and symbols—i.e., the "story" form that reality takes in our minds. If we are in our minds, we are using language, and we are invariably working with duality. If we are not in our minds, however, and instead are just resting in pure conscious awareness, then we are able to be in non-duality outside of language.

Sounds like something only Zen monks should concern themselves with, right? Thankfully, the spirit of non-duality is something we can all practice, particularly if we struggle with issues around judgment. Judgment creates distance, division, and disconnection. But dropping judgment allows us to see the fundamental nature of everything we encounter: It is whole and connected to everything else. And there is no problem.

Let's look at an example. You join a choir and find that everyone else sings better than you. You think, "They're good singers, and I'm a bad singer." Suddenly, you are separate from these other people, and you feel like something is wrong. There is automatically a problem. Maybe you feel you need to act to solve this problem. Or maybe your judgment goes the other way. Maybe you hear about a friend who was arrested for drunk driving. You think, "That's terrible. I would never, ever do something like *that*." Again, there is now distance between you and that other person, because of the judgment.

Judgment creates anxiety. You sing more quietly, shy and ashamed of your voice, in case someone hears you. You avoid the friend who was arrested, or sit and gossip about them with other friends. The anxiety, however, is an illusion, because the separateness was an illusion. There are no "good singers" and "bad singers"— these categories exist only in our minds. I'm sure many people would argue with this, but consider how many famous singers have absolutely awful-sounding voices! Consider how a musician you love could be loathed by someone else. Consider that "good singers" might one day become "bad singers," and vice versa.

With our simple division of good and bad, we have also ignored all the other shades and colors of the situation in front of us. We have knocked the nuance and dimension out of the situation and given it a narrow label (we're playing CEO again!). We ignore the fact that other people are a lot like us—that if we see brilliance in someone else, well, there is brilliance in us, too. And if we see cruelty or stupidity in others, it's in us, too. Remember that there are not two coins, just one coin with two sides. There are no good or bad people, just people with good and bad expressions and manifestations. When you can truly appreciate this, you free yourself of fixed and superficial roles. You free yourself of anxiety. You become a person—a *whole* person—simply living in the moment. Plus, you allow others to be whole, too. There is no problem.

Remember also that opposites are not in conflict—instead, they rely on one another. The rise is for the sake of the fall. The mistake is for the sake of the lesson. It's because we were hungry that we so dearly appreciate being full. So, if you notice that you are a beginner singer, you can imagine that your being a "bad singer" is simply one episode in a much longer, more complex unfolding—maybe being where you are now is precisely what allows you to practice and become a "good singer." Maybe you would not have become a good singer had you first not keenly felt how bad of a singer you were! So, there is difference, but this is not necessarily conflict. The opposites are in a relationship, not a war.

You are, in a very real way, *both* a bad singer and a good singer. If you step in with judgment and resistance, in the moment, your singing becomes a problem to solve, a riddle to understand, or a sensation to resist. If you are simply curious and accepting in the moment, then it's just you and the way you sing, and that's perfect as it is.

Without judgment and duality, you look at your friend and think, "Well, everyone has done something they're not proud of before. In another life, I can see how I could have been the one to drink and drive." You realize that just because you and your friend are currently different from one another, that doesn't mean there is a problem or that you need to react, judge, or conjure up a narrative. You realize that good people can do bad things, bad people can do good things, and that really, the present moment is continually changing and flowing anyway—who are we to interrupt it with a story of how we think it *should* be?

> One day, a farmer's son is careless and leaves the barn door open, and the horse bolts and runs away. "How unfortunate!" says the son.
>
> "Maybe, maybe not," says the farmer.
>
> The next day, the horse returns, and following it is another horse. The farmer and son now have two horses. "How fortunate!" says the son.

> "Maybe, maybe not," says the farmer.
>
> The next day, the new horse kicks the farmer's son and injures him. "I'm so unlucky!" says the son. "Maybe, maybe not," says the farmer.
>
> The next day, war breaks out in the country and the young men are drafted. The son, however, is spared because he is wounded, thus certainly saving his life. "I am the luckiest man!" says the son.
>
> "Maybe, maybe not," says the farmer . . .

When we judge, we also cut ourselves off from the flow of time. We slice out a single event or happening and look at it in isolation, then make our pronouncements. But who are we to say what role that event plays in the bigger unfolding? We cling to our ideas of what is inferior and superior, what is a good outcome and what is a bad outcome . . . but even we frequently change our minds, with time. Have you ever heard someone say something like, "At the time, my divorce was hell, but in hindsight, it was the best thing that ever happened to me"?

If we were peeking at a cat through a hole in the fence, we would see a head, then a body, then a tail, one after the other. Our experience would be that the tail followed the body, and the body followed the tail. We would see all the separate pieces. But really, there is just one single, whole cat happening all at once. It is only our narrowed vision that makes it seem like the cat is divided and unfolding as a sequential narrative.

When we call some things *good* or *bad*, we are similarly dividing up reality. We say that pain is bad and that pleasure is good. But isn't childbirth a happy kind of pain, and isn't being on heroin a bad kind of pleasure? Is "good" or "bad" really a natural feature of the rich, dynamic, full world around us, or is it just a word we made up—just a symbol or a story we tell ourselves?

Exercise 1: "There I Go . . ."

Non-duality is something best experienced rather than talked about. To feel the deeper connectedness and wholeness of the present moment, here is an exercise you can try whenever you like. Once you've tried it, though, notice if you feel the tendency to judge diminish in yourself. Also notice if you feel less tension, stress, worry, or anxiety. If you do, this exercise may be the perfect tool to whip out when you're feeling yourself getting caught in judgmental narratives and assumptions about yourself or others.

The exercise is called, "There I go . . ."

Set yourself up where you can observe people for moment (unobtrusively, of course). Maybe sit in a café or people-watch at the airport or supermarket. Let your mind go soft and receptive and simply notice who's around you. Let someone catch your attention and then notice a feature about them—perhaps even a feature you're inclined to judge or tell stories about. Let's say you notice a grumpy old woman scowling and pushing her cart through the supermarket aisles. Say to yourself, "There I go, a grumpy old lady scowling and pushing my cart." Continue for a while, but attribute what you see in the other person to yourself. "I bet my knees really hurt. I'm old now, and crabby. I'm rude to other people sometimes."

Do this with as many people as you like, and simply notice how it feels to attribute these things to yourself.

> "There I go, a happy toddler, holding my mom's hand."
>
> "There I go, a beautiful girl with a red dress on. My shoes are really uncomfortable."
>
> "There I go, a shop assistant. I'm so bored with my job and I'm waiting for my lunch break."

What's the point of this exercise? Try it and see.

When we judge, we slice the world up and make value judgments. With this exercise, though, we are doing the opposite. We are seeking connection and similarity with others, and this instantly dissolves judgment and criticism. We are feeling the wholeness of the moment rather than a fractured part of it. Sure, if you're a thirty-year-old Caucasian male, you might not have much in common with a sixty-year-old Indian mother of two . . . on the surface, at least. But when you sink into her world with compassion and curiosity, you might see that there is so much more you have in common with her than you thought.

You see that she has suffered and struggled, like you. You can see that she loves her family, like you do, and that she has many different sides to her—flaws and weaknesses—and, as a human being, her own unique flavor of beauty . . . like you!

This exercise dissolves judgment, not just for others, but for yourself, too. In time, you can look at yourself as one of the many colorful, complex, amazing citizens of the world, one of the many valued and interesting players of the unfolding saga called life, and one that deserves compassion, respect, and understanding as much as the next.

Exercise 2: The Magical Power of "And"

Duality works on the language of division, which sets *this thing* against *that thing*. Gently ease out of this mindset by using a different language; i.e., one of inclusion, addition, and totality. Watch for when you're tempted to use "but" or when you set up some people or ideas against others. Watch when you do this for aspects of yourself; i.e., some parts are good, *but* some parts are bad. Then, when you notice yourself doing this, try loosening that tension in your mind by reframing it with the magical word "and". Here are a few examples.

"I absolutely love cooking, but I don't know a thing about baking" becomes "I love cooking, and I'm less knowledgeable about baking." See the difference? It's subtle, but the "and" keeps both these attributes together in one, unproblematic whole, rather than playing them off against each other.

"You think we should go tomorrow, but I disagree" becomes "You think we should go tomorrow, and I think today's better." The difference is still there . . . but there's somehow less conflict.

"I really wanted him to make the first move on our date last night, but he was so shy!" becomes "I wanted him to make the first move, and he was really shy and reluctant." There is now no problem between the eagerness and the shyness—they are just two things happening together.

You don't need to literally use the word "and" to capture this essence, though. In time, you can hone your ears to notice all the ways you use language to create division—and instead choose to use words that express wholeness or make enough room for differences to exist without judgment, ranking, interpretation, or "shoulds".

Notice, for example, when you feel judgmental of a friend who's just had her fifth child, despite constantly struggling for money. Where does this judgy, superior, critical feeling come from? Look inside and see that you have made divisions—good moms versus bad moms, rich people versus poor people, smart people versus idiots, and on and on. Now, see if you can simply allow those differences to exist without your story or interpretation or judgment. Your friend is broke. She now has five children. That's it. There is no problem.

Clear away your need to attach value to her situation (and yours!) and simply see her for what she is. She's broke and she has five children. Is that something you need to go to war against? In fact, can you potentially find how these two positions are not in as much conflict as you might initially think, and that you don't need to rush in with your ego and make a pronouncement about good and bad, or should and shouldn't?

"This is my friend, and I love her to pieces. She hasn't got two pennies to rub together. They're expecting their fifth child; it's a mad house over there! But there's nobody quite like her in this world, and though I didn't make those choices, *she* did. And I love her!"

Being non-judgmental is about so, so much more than "live and let live." In fact, you are not required to "let" anyone do anything, and nothing in reality needs your permission or approval to carry on as it will. Isn't that relieving? And isn't it so much easier to appreciate the moment for what it is when you're not playing "reality-police"? The secret to being cool, calm, collected, serene, and completely at peace with yourself is this: Reality can be trusted to be what it is, and all we are required to do is live in the moment and be as we are.

Takeaways

- Anxiety and overthinking often come from our tendency to judge ourselves, others, situations, and life itself. If we can reduce our habit of labeling, criticizing, or using black-and-white, us-versus-them thinking, then we can reduce tension and anxiety and increase our ability to be compassionate and accepting.
- To be less judgmental, we can focus on how people (including ourselves) really are in the moment, rather than clinging to our memories, stories, interpretations, or judgments about them.

People's temporary behavior is not the same as their absolute, unchanging essence!

- To drop our judgmental inner narratives, we can turn our focus to "just the facts" and realize that without judgment and divisive language, there is no conflict and no need to go to war with what is.
- Don't assume, interpret, expect, or mind-read. Instead, be in the moment and perceive it as it is.
- Many of us judge ourselves because we make comparisons between what we think *should* be and what is. The key to self-acceptance and serenity is not to match up our ideal self with our perceived, inadequate self—rather, it is to drop the ideal self and accept how we actually are. We can notice and make room for our experience, *whatever it is.* This will bring deep calm and confidence that goes beyond achievement, ego, or self-esteem.
- The Buddhist concept of non-duality teaches that suffering comes from the illusory splitting and dividing of reality, which, although it consists of opposites, is not at war with itself. When we appreciate the wholeness and connectedness of everything in life, we are less tempted to sit in judgment, to divide into categories of good and bad, or to make definitive pronouncements. We are able to "hold" difference and uncertainty without going into resistance or problem-solving mode.

- If we notice judgment in ourselves, we can dissolve it by using less divisive language or actively seeking similarities between us and the people we pretend are against us.

Summary Guide

CHAPTER 1: IT'S ALL IN THE PERSPECTIVE

- The biggest difference between those who are anxious and those who aren't might be the difference between being *proactive* and *reactive.* To be proactive is to hold the perspective that you are in charge of and responsible for your life, and create conditions as you will them rather than react to conditions created by others.
- There are many ways to make this mindset shift. Firstly, commit to dropping blaming others or complaining about situations without taking action. If you notice yourself passively whining or resenting others, ask, "*What action can I personally take to change my situation?*"
- Change and difficulty is inevitable, but we can practice being flexible, creative, and solution-oriented rather than getting bogged down by things not going our way. This reduces anxiety.

- We can be more proactive when we stop daydreaming or thinking about "one day" or "if only"—again, we can take inspired action, right now, to empower ourselves.
- To gain a calm, proactive mindset, we can practice putting some distance between us and any strong emotions or thoughts we have. With psychological distance, we gain a broader perspective and empower ourselves to become conscious of our thoughts as thoughts, thus making space to choose consciously and proactively. By creating spatial, temporal, or hypothetical distance, we are no longer at the mercy of external events, but have an internal locus of control.
- Our imaginations can also help us gain much-needed distance and clarity. You can imagine yourself advising a friend to see a fresh perspective on an issue. You can also visualize another version of yourself to entertain other possibilities and alternatives. Finally, you can practice reframing perceptions and notice how you think and feel without attaching any stories, value judgments, or resistance to that awareness. This alone brings calm, but also opens up a space for a new perspective to emerge.

CHAPTER 2: STEPPING OFF THE CAROUSEL

- When it comes to anxiety rumination, and overthinking, mindfulness practices can help if they are tethered to concrete action in the moment, as outlined in the ACT model. In acceptance and commitment therapy, we accept what we cannot control and commit to taking action to change the things we can according to our personal values in order to improve our lives.

- In ACT, anxiety is often about experiential avoidance, which we can counteract using the six core principles.
- The first is to genuinely contact the present without judgment, interpretation, resistance, or narrative, but with conscious alertness and open curiosity about what is unfolding in the now.
- The second is cognitive defusion, where we separate out our thoughts about reality from reality itself. We accept our thoughts as thoughts so we don't get tangled up in them. The third is acceptance, where we welcome and acknowledge reality without arguing with it. We don't have to agree or condone, only observe. We use the fourth concept, the observing self, to have a conscious "meta" perspective on our thoughts. One part is having an experience, while another part is observing us having that experience.
- The fifth is to find our values and principles so that we can put our thoughts into context. The observing self can appraise our thoughts and compare them against our values so we can do the sixth principle—take conscious, inspired action.

- The acronym ACT can help us: Accept your internal experience in the present moment, choose a valued direction, and take action in that direction. This reduces anxiety and overthinking.
- Overcoming anxious rumination is about learning to identify it. Compared to normal cognition, rumination is endless, doesn't bring insight, and doesn't actually improve anything, even though it temporarily feels like problem-solving.
- "Challenging your thoughts" isn't necessary and only plays into further experiential avoidance and resistance. Instead, ask if a thought is useful and whether it's helping you achieve goals in accordance with your values. Compassion, forgiveness, and the 3M strategy (meet, make, move) are also great strategies for empowering yourself out of rumination.
- There is a mantra called the 4 A's of stress management. These are avoid, alter, accept, and adapt. Avoiding things entails simply walking away from things you can't control. Some things are just not worth the effort and are best removed from our environments altogether. However, if we can't avoid it, we must learn how to alter our environment to remove the stressor. If we can't alter our environment, we have no choice but to accept it. Lastly, if we can't do much about the situation at all, we must adapt to it and learn how to cope with our stressor and reduce its damaging potential to a minimum.

CHAPTER 3: THE ART OF COGNITIVE RESTRUCTURING

- Once we are firmly in our accepting, aware "observing self," we can begin to rethink our cognitive distortions, expectations, inner myths and narratives, assumptions, and biases. We don't *challenge* them, exactly, but make space for alternatives that we choose consciously.
- We can practice cognitive restructuring by first becoming aware of the way we think and shining consciousness onto what has been previously automatic, habitual and unconscious. When we can shift our perspective and gently change our self-concept, we start to think, feel, and behave differently, and this change is not superficial or mere "positive thinking."
- After awareness, we can adjust, dispute, or engage with our thoughts and consciously choose alternatives. We can then play these alternatives out in our real lives. We do not need to judge ourselves, fix anything, or find out the "truth," but instead appraise our thoughts according to how useful they are in achieving our goals, set in accordance to our deepest values.
- The two-column technique can help us slow down, identify automatic negative thoughts, and restructure them consciously. This takes patience, courage, compassion, and curiosity. Look for all-or-nothing thinking, catastrophizing, mind-

reading, trying to predict the future, making generalizations, or extreme negative appraisals. Reword these thoughts or even consider how they may be converted into useful action.

- There are countless techniques for cognitive restructuring, but they all begin with awareness and end with our willingness to genuinely entertain alternatives. We can use Socratic questioning (keep asking after evidence for assumptions and beliefs, keep asking why), guided imagery (to rehearse or flesh out alternatives, past or future), record-keeping or journaling (to put thoughts down and play around with alternatives), and experimenting with "what-if?" (to follow catastrophizing to its logical conclusion and see if discomfort, failure, or uncertainty are really all that bad).
- Cognitive restructuring can help us cultivate a perspective and mindset that is proactive and less anxiety-filled by design.

CHAPTER 4: ALL WE HAVE IS NOW

- Panic, worry, rumination, anxiety, and overthinking can stem from over-identifying with the inner mental chatter and narratives we have about life, which are often filled with cognitive distortions, biases, illusory expectations, fears, and sheer irrationality. Our brain can conjure up stressful mental activity in the past or the future, but calmness and serenity only occur in one place: the present.

- All we have is now. Surrender, acceptance, and calm awareness in the present doesn't mean we are passive or giving up—if we can act, we act. If we can't, we accept it. There is no need for anxiety or rumination. Remember that anxiety and overthinking don't actually solve problems for us or help us in any way, even if our brain convinces us that we need to rush in and control everything.
- Getting comfortable with the present moment means practicing patience, humility, humor, tolerance of the uncertain, and flexibility to respond to the moment rather than react to or resist it.
- Pain is inevitable and fleeting. But suffering is in our response to pain, and is avoidable. If we cling to pain by resisting it, telling stories about it, or repeatedly pulling it back into the moment from the past, we are creating suffering for ourselves. Calm, proactive people accept pain and let it pass and don't allow themselves to get caught up in unnecessary suffering.
- Your physical body, your five senses, and your conscious awareness are anchors in the present moment. You can be in the Here and Now rather than Elsewhere whenever you anchor into the present moment via the body. Still a busy mind by moving your body (such as with physical

activity), or do sensory meditation to slow down and connect to the present again.

CHAPTER 5: THERE IS NO BLACK AND WHITE

- Anxiety and overthinking often come from our tendency to judge ourselves, others, situations, and life itself. If we can reduce our habit of labeling, criticizing, or using black-and-white, us-versus-them thinking, then we can reduce tension and anxiety and increase our ability to be compassionate and accepting.
- To be less judgmental, we can focus on how people (including ourselves) really are in the moment, rather than clinging to our memories, stories, interpretations, or judgments about them. People's temporary behavior is not the same as their absolute, unchanging essence!
- To drop our judgmental inner narratives, we can turn our focus to "just the facts" and realize that without judgment and divisive language, there is no conflict and no need to go to war with what is.
- Don't assume, interpret, expect, or mind-read. Instead, be in the moment and perceive it as it is.
- Many of us judge ourselves because we make comparisons between what we think *should* be and what is. The key to self-acceptance and serenity is not to match up our ideal self with our perceived, inadequate self—rather, it is to drop the ideal self and accept how we actually are. We can notice

and make room for our experience, *whatever it is.* This will bring deep calm and confidence that goes beyond achievement, ego, or self-esteem.

- The Buddhist concept of non-duality teaches that suffering comes from the illusory splitting and dividing of reality, which, although it consists of opposites, is not at war with itself. When we appreciate the wholeness and connectedness of everything in life, we are less tempted to sit in judgment, to divide into categories of good and bad, or to make definitive pronouncements. We are able to "hold" difference and uncertainty without going into resistance or problem-solving mode.
- If we notice judgment in ourselves, we can dissolve it by using less divisive language or actively seeking similarities between us and the people we pretend are against us.